TOURISTS IN THE COUNTRY OF LOVE

a Book of Short Fiction

by

Jo Rousseau

REaDLIPS Press

Editor: Noreen Lace

Cover Art: Flora Westbrook

Copyright © 2020 ReadLips Press
Los Angeles, Ca.

All Rights Reserved: No part of this book in whole or in part shall be reproduced without written permission from author and publisher.

This is a work of fiction. Any part reflecting persons or events is coincidental.

ISBN: **978-1-7331813-4-1**
LCCN:

Love is the triumph of imagination over intelligence.

                                          H.L. Mencken

Note to Readers:

These stories are about how we go on. In the story, "Statues in a Blue Garden," Georgette Landau is visited by a once-upon-a-time beau whom she had secreted in her heart for fifty years. A loving husband and privileged life in Paris had not erased the memory of the heart-pounding excitement of first love. Even though abandoned by this beau, the magic of first love could not be dispelled. Georgette had gone on with her life and now she is presented with the return of her first love.

How do we go on after we've lost a parent? How do we go on when our family is broken with no means to repair it? Sondra Hendricks, her brother, Vincent, and sister, Laura, face just this question in "Reading to my Mother." Help and strength come from surprising places and life stumbles along riddled with uncertainty.

How do we go on when our society is changing around us at whirlwind speed? How do we achieve traction in the world, how do we hang on to what we love when what we love is no longer valued except by a few? Cynthia Carter must navigate this tricky terrain in "The Book Finder." Desperately trying to preserve a tradition of the physical world of books, Cynthia fights against her society in this futuristic story.

All the characters, of course, find a way to go on—at least temporarily. But, the battle for survival, for peace and happiness, is a minefield. Shakespeare may have opined that the world is a stage, but he didn't warn us about the myriad trapdoors ready to spring without notice.

The stories in this book are about love in its many permutations. Love holds eternal curiosity, eternal mystery; we love love in all its confusing, heart-shattering euphoria. I hope you read with pleasure.

Jo Rousseau

TABLE OF CONTENTS

Reading to my Mother	1
Statues in a Blue Garden	50
Johnsonville	71
Aunt Tilly's Cure for Heartbreak	91
The Book Finder	100
The Last Race	135
36 Views of X	155
Maurissa takes the F-Scale	172
Moving to Jupiter's Moons	180
Comrades	218
Love's Actuary	234
Siberia	253
The Island in Winter	288

Jo Rousseau

Reading to my Mother

At times, I thought my mother was asleep or even that she'd slipped peacefully away and then, as I paused in the reading to look for jumpy movement behind her closed eyes, she'd snort and ask why I'd stopped. She would lie in her hospital bed, her eyes closed, her breathing so shallow that I could hardly perceive it, and she would say in her hoarse whisper, "Go on." It was embarrassing. Not my mother dying in her hospital bed, not her tubes and monitors or the smell of ammonia and dry, stale breath, but what she'd asked me to read. I'd brought *The Complete Works of Mark Twain* but she would have none of it. "Are you trying to bore me to death, Sondra?" she admonished me weakly, "Read the Nabokov," meaning passages she'd marked in *Lolita,* passages that she knew by heart. She smiled vaguely, her lips moving silently to the words I read. She would complain if I stopped when a nurse or doctor came in, "Don't stop!" she'd bark in a commanding voice, surprising me with her sudden strength. It embarrassed me, but I read on.

My father and brother were allowed to read their own selections to her, even when, to my mother's annoyance, my father insisted on reading *A la Recherché du Temps Perdu* in his mangled, indecipherable French. "It helps her sleep," he insisted gently as though, as always, he knew exactly what she needed. When I replied that of course she went to sleep, she didn't know French and she was bored to tears, he remarked, "Oh, pooh. Don't be a twit, Sondra! Lizzy is used to being bored!"

My father at eighty-two was still strong and straight-backed. He walked four miles a day with his ancient sheep dog, Minos, and he ate whatever he wanted including his special fire-hot chili that instantly turned my own stomach to one flaming cauldron of acid. He came to read right after lunch, I came about five-thirty after I got off work, and Vincent came at the stroke of seven to stay with her for the last two visiting hours. Vincent taught poetry at the University and Mother didn't raise any objection at all when he read obscure Rilke verses. "It doesn't matter. My son's voice soothes me," she said when I asked her why she allowed that.

Laura never came.

My father and brother brought their books in with them and took them out again, but the ones I read to my mother were kept in her hospital nightstand. It wasn't hardcore pornography but a kind of elegant literary pornography that Mother had always secretly enjoyed. Her books were littered with bookmarks that had been in place for decades. She had brought four books with her and we'd already been through passages from Nabokov's *Lolita,* Miller's *Tropic of Capricorn*, and, my personal favorite, Elkin's bear scene from *The Making of Ashenden*. Now, she had asked for Nin's *The Delta of Venus*.

At home, my mother's office was tucked in what, at the turn of the century, would have been the maid's room. She had a comfy chair with a reading lamp, a small desk and wall-to-wall, ceiling-to-floor books. Most evenings, she was nestled in her room while my father read in his more spacious office on the first floor—a room that had at one time been a parlor. I had grown up with my mother and father's books so they held as much interest for me as the labels on soup cans. Separate books in separate rooms made for little conversation. My father, only accidentally cruel, would say, "Why would I talk to your mother when I can talk to Heidegger or Kierkegaard?" I didn't answer him, only thought that maybe a good reason was because she could provide conversation outside his own head. People, even his children, seemed a socially necessary hindrance to his time with his books.

"Start on page three." My mother raised a hand as if she were pointing out the passage to me, one thin finger lifted toward the yellowed book I cradled in my hands.

I almost dreaded it, but Mother seemed to take such pleasure and, well, she was dying. What could I do?

"Seeing the penis go into her magnificent mouth between her flashing teeth," I read, "while her breasts heaved, gave men a pleasure for which they paid generously."

"No, no! Further up. The paragraph before," my mother instructed. "Then, re-read that part."

Sometimes my mother would make little sounds and I wasn't sure if it was because of some sudden pain or if the passage had brought back pleasurable memories of my father, time spent together in the bedroom. Maybe he found reason to talk to her then. Even so, it was difficult to imagine my mother engaging in oral sex with my father, hard to see them sharing passion of any kind other than a passion for the written word. They were my parents, for goodness sake, and I had always seen them as dull bookworms.

My mother continued to instruct me on what passages to read, where to start, asking me to re-read ones that she particularly liked. It was a side of her I hadn't suspected; I was in awe that, at her age, she still found such pleasure in this.

I hadn't notice that Dr. Patterson half-entered the room and stood in the doorway with a perplexed look on his face. When I realized he was there, I stopped reading, feeling the heat as my face flushed.

"Why are you stopping? I'm not dead yet!" my mother complained irritably.

Dr. Patterson walked to the side of her bed. "How are you today, Elizabeth?"

"I was fine until you interrupted us," my mother scowled at him. "My blood was just starting to get a head of steam. My heart could stand to beat a little faster from time to time."

"I'll recommend…uh.." Dr. Patterson tipped the book in my hands to see the title, "I'll recommend pornography for all my patients," Dr. Patterson grinned looking at me for the first time. He lifted my mother's fragile arm to take her pulse; then he scanned her chart. "I wish these charts were as interesting."

"When can I go home?" my mother asked as she had every day for the past ten days, her voice gone childlike. Dr. Patterson had already turned his back to leave.

"We'll see," he told her.

"Pornography!" my mother spit out when the doctor was out of earshot. "It's erotic literature! Erotica! What does he know? He's only a medical doctor, not a doctor of arts and letters. Hmph! Go to page one-thirty-six, the lesbian love scene between Elena and Leila."

How many times had she read this? When did she start? Had it been part of her relationship with my father?

"Her tongue between Elena's legs" I read, "was like a stabbing, agile and sharp. When the orgasm came, it was so vibrant that it shook their bodies from head to foot."

Then, I could see him. Dr. Patterson outside the door listening to me read. Next to the door was a glass panel with a gauze curtain and I could see his dark shape through the glass. This time I wasn't mortified.

It was almost time for Vincent to appear and I could hardly wait. I'd had quite enough of my mother's literary licentiousness. As soon as I'd stopped reading, Dr. Patterson's shadow disappeared.

"Can I get you anything, Mom?" She didn't answer and I suspected that she had fallen asleep. I put the book back in the nightstand. I had been sitting for almost an hour and a half, so I got up to stretch my legs. Mom's room was private, thank God, with a window that overlooked a city park. The streetlights had come on so ribbons of light cut across the darkness of the trees. I was still standing there when Vincent came in.

"Hi, sis. How's mom doing?" Vincent was still carrying his book bag. He'd walked across the park from the University.

"You know, it's hard to say."

"Has the doctor been in to see her?"

I nodded. "He didn't really say much. She's dying, Vincent." I shook my head and shrugged.

"I heard that!" My mother's voice was

shattered with coughing that shook her to her fragile bones. "What does he know? He doesn't know anything. What's his name?"

My heart sank that I'd let her hear me say that, but Vincent was laughing.

"You tell'em, Mom!" he chuckled. "You're going to keep going until you're a hundred!"

"Dr. Patterson," I said. "His name is Dr. Patterson." Then to Vincent, "Do you want me to sit with you awhile?"

"No, I imagine you've had enough of this place for one day." He came over and kissed me on the cheek. "I guess Laura hasn't shown her face?"

I shook my head again, then turned to my mother and kissed her on the forehead. "See you tomorrow, Mom."

"Ah, well, maybe." I looked at her as if to ask where she thought she might be going but before I could ask she continued, "I'm dying, you know."

"Don't even joke," I said kissing her again. "I love you, Mom."

"I love you too," she whispered, "And I love Laura too. Tell her if I don't get the chance."

Vincent was drawing out his book of poems, taking the seat that I had vacated. I could hear his voice grow fainter and fainter as I walked down the hall toward the elevators.

Outside the hospital, a cold wind had whipped up. As I drew my coat collar up around my neck, I saw a figure off to the side, stamping her feet and smoking nervously. At first, I thought it was only some fool who preferred to smoke even if it was ten degrees outside than to try to quit, but then I recognized the figure as Laura. When she realized it was me, she turned away.

"Laura?" I called out to her. I didn't know whether I was outraged or relieved. "Why are you standing out here in the cold?" I hadn't seen my sister for six years but we didn't embrace, and we didn't kiss. I knew how much Laura hated being touched. She pulled her over-sized coat around her. She wore men's boots; those were over-sized as well as though she had dressed from a man's closet. Unkempt hair sprayed from under a stocking cap. Laura dropped her cigarette and twisted the butt into the sidewalk. She pushed her hands into her coat pockets and shrugged.

"Is she alone?" my sister asked.

"You mean is Dad up there?" She hadn't spoken to our father since she was eighteen, twenty years ago or more. "No," I told her. "Vincent is with her right now. You should go up. She misses you so much. She loves you."

Laura stamped her feet, the thick work boots cracking sharply on the frozen concrete. She lit another cigarette. "Nah, I can't go up like this. I need a shower."

"Buy you a cup of coffee? The hospital has a coffee shop. Let's go in. I'm freezing!"

Laura took another long drag. "I'm all dirty, Sondra. I'll embarrass you."

"Don't be crazy. I'm glad to see you. I want to talk. Besides, the cafeteria light is dim. Everybody looks dirty." I held the door open and led her into the warmth of the cafeteria. "Grab a table," I told her. "I'll get us some coffee. You want a sandwich or something?'

I poured the cups of coffee and stood in the cashier's line looking at Laura who was looking down at a container of creamer that she turned around in her hands. She was a mess, all right, but she looked healthy. Her eyes seemed clear and wide-open. Her skin was hardly youthful and her hair, which looked cut by her own hand, was matted and flat where her cap had been.

"Why don't you take off your coat?" I set the coffee in front of her. She poured in as much cream as the cup would hold.

"Remember that cat Mom had? Sorrow." It was typical of Laura not to respond but to follow the train of thought she was already in the midst of. "It was the oddest-looking little cat. Looked like someone had thrown it together with pieces of about a dozen cats. Yellow, black, white, grey." I was beginning to remember as Laura talked. "And I told Mom she ought to name it Sorrowful, not just Sorrow. The cat was on her lap and she was stroking it so lovingly and she said, 'No, this cat is Sorrow.' It was like the cat *was* her sorrow, Mom's sorrow, and she stroked that sorrow and cooed to it to soothe herself."

"Mom doesn't have long, Laura. You ought to go up." I didn't mean to interrupt. Badgering didn't work with Laura, but if Mom was going to see her middle-child again, the sooner the better. "Are you still in the shelter? I left messages."

"Messages? Yes, yes, of course I got your messages. I'm here."

I'd lost confidence long ago that Laura was telling me the truth. She seemed to take a kind of pride in lying to me, mocking lies as though I were hopelessly naïve or too ridiculously polite to call her out. "Are you getting medication?"

Laura frowned. "You sound like Dad."

I wish our conversation could be different but I needed to know the basics. Laura would see it as prying, I knew that, but I had to get her up to

Mom's room, let Mom see Laura's face again before it was too late. I was afraid I was driving Laura away, though, rather than drawing her in. I didn't know how to talk to her.

"Look who it is!" Vincent was suddenly at our table. "Stand up so I can give you a hug!"

Laura did this reluctantly. Even as a child she shied away from physical affection. Now, though, she smelled of the streets, her fingernails were ragged and dirty. It wasn't shyness so much as shame.

I scooted over and Vincent slid in next to me, Laura across the table. "Mom's asleep for a minute, so I got to get right back. Just needed some coffee. This is the last week of school before final exams and the students can be absolutely brutal."

I smiled at him, pushed my untouched cup his way. He pulled it in front of him, willingly accepting it. Laura stared at him quizzically. No doubt she was thinking of Vincent's use of the word brutal, as though it was doubtful that teaching poetry and brutality were concepts that could exist in the same world.

"You look good!" Vincent told her.

"You're so full of crap, Vincent." She gave his shoulder an aw-gee, schoolgirl's nudge. "Can I smoke in here?"

Vincent laughed. He laughed often and I was glad of it, made me feel happy. I shook my head. "Come up," I begged her.

"I gotta go." Laura clutched the half-empty paper cup. "I'll come back tomorrow after I get cleaned up. I don't want her to see…"

"It won't matter, Laura. She wants to see you. It doesn't matter." But Laura was out of the booth mumbling over her shoulder that she'd see us tomorrow. I didn't imagine that she would though.

The evenings at home seemed quiet and I carried the hospital room with me. Mom's room was there when I ate dinner, when I soaked in a hot bath, when I finally crawled between cold sheets. It was there all through work the next day; the hospital smell would suddenly be in my nostrils, the feel of the paper I shuffled like the feel of the books I read to her. Somehow, driving to the hospital again after work, the cold air, the too warm heat coming through the vents, sent a wave of nausea over me. Once again in Mom's room, my dad slept in the chair and my mom in her hospital bed. I came in as quietly as I could and sat in the closest chair to look at them. Dying is hard; I could see that. The habit of living wants to hold no matter what. My mother looked smaller every day, lying now in a bed that she seemed to sink deeper and deeper into. Her IVs were gone and it looked as though she was also free of the heart monitor. A nurse came in with my mother's dinner tray not long after I sat down. She jiggled my mother's shoulder gently and my mother, groggy, disoriented, looked at my father and asked, "Is he dead?"

"No, Mom. At least I don't think so. He just fell asleep."

"Well, wake him up, Laura. It scares me to see him like that."

She'd called me Laura. She hadn't done that since the two of us were small, always calling one by the other's name in her haste to prevent us from one fatal mistake or another. Now, it gave me pause. "I'm Sondra, Mom." I guess in an attempt to suppress anger, I settled for too much whine in my voice; life is not a rehearsal. The lines we speak are the lines we speak. I couldn't take the words back. Dealing with my mother's fragile body was one thing, but I wasn't sure I could deal with a fragile mind. Her calling me by my sister's name scared me.

"I know who you are, Sondra. Wake your father."

I fluffed her pillow, moved her tray over her lap, took off the lid to her soup, and unwrapped her utensils.

"Dad?" I called across Mom's bed. "Dad, I'm here. You can go home now." My father didn't stir and I went around the bed to rouse him. They were old, my parents, and their faces, when asleep, did look dead, the flesh of their faces saggy and ashen. I wanted desperately for them to see Laura before it was too late. Too late…I always put it that way. I took his hand, rubbed the length of his arm, and he turned, disoriented at first.

"Lizzy, you okay?" I didn't know if he was looking at me, if he knew where he was, but he sat up in the chair he'd been slouched in.

"Mom's okay," I assured him. "She's getting ready to eat something. You should go home and do the same."

He nodded. Dad pushed himself up, rocked a bit, and managed to get to his feet after the third try. He stretched a little until he looked like his hale and hearty self, and started putting on his coat. He shuffled over and kissed Mom on her forehead. She didn't look up from her soup or say goodbye when he shuffled out of the room.

"Why don't you read something, Sondra?"

My mother had read to us from the time I

could remember, every night sitting on the edge of our bed. When we got older, she'd read to us at lunch from a newspaper or magazines, things we didn't understand at the time but that prepared us to understand. As I think about it, I can't remember a real conversation. Surely, there were conversations. When I think of her, she is reading to us, to herself, to her students, to anyone who would listen really.

"What would you like, Mom?"

"How about a change of pace? There's a bible in that drawer." She cast her head in the direction of the drawer.

The Bible? Really? Had she found some racy verses in *The Bible*?

"Nothing funereal. No 'though I walk through the valley of the shadow of death' nonsense. Read something cheery."

Something cheery from *The Bible*? People turn to stone, get thrown into the lion's den, drown in floods. Is there anything cheery? "Cheery?" I asked her, "In *The Bible?*"

"Okay, maybe not cheery. Inspirational maybe. Hopeful. Maybe something about miracles, impossible cures, or being raised from the dead. That's in there somewhere." She poked her spoon into the air.

I didn't know my way around *The Bible* and all I could think of was something about the lilies of the field and I had no clue where to find that verse. I found a "fear not" verse in *Joshua* and many "shall not" verses in the *New Testament*, but none of them seemed to please my mother. She was restless and had pushed her dinner tray away having eaten less than half of it.

"Oh, stop that and talk to me, Laura," she said grumpily.

Maybe a conversation? All I said was "I'm Sondra, Mom."

"Oh, for... What's the difference? Don't be so picky!"

I have to admit to pouting, to absolute head-hanging sulking. I was there. Maybe I should read the passage about the prodigal son?

"Okay, talk to me, *Sondra*." She emphasized my name. Maybe I was making a big deal out of nothing, but I didn't think so.

"Since we're on the topic of Laura," I wasn't convinced I should tell her, but I went on, "I saw her last night and wanted her to come up, but she wouldn't. Embarrassed about how she looked—at least that's what she said. I told her it wouldn't matter to you, that you just wanted to see her."

"No, it wouldn't have mattered. Is she okay?"

Dr. Patterson came striding through the door, approached Mother's bed, coming to a sharp stop beside it. He picked up the napkin Mom had thrown over her food to take a look. "No appetite?" he asked her.

Mom just shrugged. She'd eaten more than usual. "Who can eat that?"

Dr. Patterson looked at me. "What are you reading today?"

"*The Bible*," I told him.

He laughed. "No, really. What are you reading?"

"*The Bible*…really."

He seemed disappointed.

"I have good news, Elizabeth. You may be able to go home tomorrow. You want to go home, don't you?"

His words shocked me. I'd assumed Mom would spend her last days here and that these were, in fact, her last days. Now she was nodding her head vigorously at the doctor, letting him know that, yes, she was ready to be home.

"Well," the Doctor went on, "that's the good news. The bad news is there's really nothing more we can do. There's no treatment that will help you. I want you to consider palliative care at home. Not hospice, no, not yet… palliative."

Directing his next comments to me, he said, "Do you live with your mother?"

"She lives with my dad. He's pretty strong, but I don't know that he can care for her."

"Of course he can care for me! I practically wiped his ass for him for close to fifty years; he can wipe mine for a little while now."

Dr Patterson laughed. "Yes, I think she's strong enough to go home." He took her pulse and listened to her heart, stopping, cocking his head to the side, listening again. "I'll send someone in to talk to you…fill out some papers. Did you get out of bed today? Can you walk to the bathroom?"

"It's five steps to the bathroom, for goodness sake. I get up and go when I'm ready. Oh, I follow the rules, Doctor, and call the nurse so that she'll be here if I fall, but I haven't fallen and I won't fall. I'm pretty steady on my feet. And, there's a walker at home if I need it. I'll be fine. Better, in fact. I'll die in here. Let me go home."

Dr. Patterson wasn't smiling anymore. "Look, Elizabeth, I want you to go home; you should go home. I do think you'll do better. Your appetite will improve." Looking toward me, then, "How far do you live from your parents? You can look in on her?" He didn't wait for me to answer. "Well, a woman will come and take the information, see what you need, see how the house is set up, interview the husband. Make sure he can handle it."

"He can handle it!" my mother yelled. "Alfred's going to live forever and he's strong as an ox. Don't worry about me. My husband can take care of me."

"What time is Alfred usually here?"

"Right after lunch. The man is as regular as the tide," Mom beamed.

She was happy to be going home. "She's right. Dad is in good health," I told the doctor. "I'll be here too and maybe Vincent. Tomorrow's Saturday."

"Tomorrow's Saturday again? How long have I been in here?"

"Ten days, Mom."

When Vincent came in Mom was anxious to tell him the "good" news, but Vincent knew right away that going home meant the end days were here. Hospitals, in his opinion didn't want dying patients to mess up their statistics.

"That's great, Mom." Vincent kissed her cheek and hugged her as best he could. "Does Dad know?"

I wanted to talk to Vincent alone, away from Mom but it didn't look like I was going to get the chance right now. We were so used to functioning without Laura that I normally wouldn't have thought about her for help, but we needed her if she wasn't strung out or manic. I had hopes from the looks of her. Vincent had heard her say she'd come today but so far, no sign. No big surprise.

When his back was to Mom, Vincent mouthed, "Laura?" I shook my head.

Outside the hospital, I looked around for my sister not really expecting to see her. It had started to snow lightly. It wasn't sticking but blowing in swirls in the streets and in the L-shaped alcoves of the building. I hurried to my car, got in, turned on the heater as high as it would go, and waited for the car to warm up. If Mom went home tomorrow, I'd have to help, maybe get Dad to drive the car up to the door so that she'd be in the cold the shortest time possible. And, I had to make sure there were groceries in the house. Lots of soup. Dad could warm soup. They'd be okay. They had each other and me and Vincent and good insurance. We could do without Laura. If they needed someone to come in, they could afford it. They'd be okay, I told myself again. They'd be okay.

I barely had time to feed my cat before I was on my way to the hospital a little before noon the next day. It was freezing and traces of snow drew white lines around the bases of the trees and the edges of the sidewalk. I was the first to arrive. Mom was animated, excited at the possibility of going home. She told me that she had wanted to get dressed and gather her things for her suitcase, but the nurse said she needed to stay in bed until the release was signed. She told me that she hadn't seen Dr. Patterson yet that morning but someone would sign the release if he wasn't there.

"Get my books out of the bed table, Sondra. They might kill the next patient."

I did as I was told but then didn't know what to do with them. I sat there with the books on my lap until I just set them by my feet on the floor. A little after noon, Vincent came in.

"Where's Dad?"

"Your dad will be here. Probably had to stop at the men's room. He can't go from the kitchen to the bedroom without stopping to pee." Mom rolled her eyes.

We waited. Mom's lunch came. She took one look at it and decided that she'd wait until she got home to eat. Vincent convinced her, though, that she ought to eat something while it was hot or at least eat the fruit cup. It would take a while, he told her, to process the papers.

At twelve-thirty, Dad still wasn't there. What had Mom said? As regular as the tide? It was only thirty minutes, but I was worried. I called his cell but there was no answer. That wasn't unusual. He went a lifetime with no phone in his pocket and he was always leaving it somewhere or other. Maybe it was in his shirt pocket when he did the wash or maybe he'd left it in the car. Anyway, again, there was nothing unusual in his not answering. On the other hand, he could have slipped on ice getting into the car or lost control of the car on a slick patch, or a dozen other horrors I could think of. Still I thought that he was bound to come walking through the door any minute so I was reluctant to leave to go look for him. Vincent was getting antsy, though, and ready to act.

He looked at his watch. "If Dad isn't here in fifteen minutes, I'm going looking for him."

"He's as steady as a rock. Nothing can happen to your father." Mom was sure. She was counting on it. Fifteen minutes came and went. Vincent put on his coat. "I'll be back," he said.

The woman we were all supposed to meet stepped in, but when we told her we weren't ready, she promised to come back in an hour.

I could tell Mom was agitated. She didn't want me to read; her concentration was shot. She just kept saying over and over, "Where could he be?" or "Alfred, where are you?" Neither one of us could let our minds settle.

"Vincent will get him, Mom. Dad probably just forgot what day it is."

But Dad wouldn't forget. He didn't forget what day it was or the list of things he had to do in a day. He wasn't late…ever. Something was wrong.

"Maybe the car wouldn't start," I said to Mom. "It's really cold outside."

Mom seemed to calm, not because she bought this latest explanation I don't think, but just because there was nothing left to do or say.

Then, my phone rang. It was Vincent.

"Step out of the room," was the first thing he said. It was bad. It was going to be bad.

"I'm out," I told him.

"I came in and Dad was lying on the floor in his bedroom. He's not breathing, Sondra."

"Vincent, that can't be right. Are you sure? Did you call 911?"

"He's all dressed. It looks like he just turned around to go downstairs and out the door to the hospital. Instead, he just…. He can't have been lying here very long. It doesn't look like he tried to move or get up after he went down—I mean the bed isn't mussed from his trying to pull himself up and the carpet has no marks where he might have dragged himself."

"Vincent, did you call 911?"

"Yes. I'm waiting for them now."

Vincent was so calm, like he always is. He wasn't just calm on the outside, like me, but truly calm on the inside. My knees went a little weak and I leaned against the wall for support; on the other side of the wall, my mom was waiting for my father, ready for him to take her home. "What am I going to tell Mom?"

"The truth."

I thought about this no more than a second. "I'll wait for you." I couldn't process this news. I couldn't imagine.

"I don't know how long I'll be. I don't know what happens now. If they want to take him directly to a funeral home, which one should I tell them?" We were both silent a minute and then Vincent went on, "I guess that's Mom's decision. You'll have to tell her. She's the one who can make the decision."

Then, I saw her: Laura walking down the hall toward me. She looked good. She looked like anybody else walking down the hall toward her mother's hospital room. Wait. It was anybody else.

The woman turned into another room and, for a split second, I thought that Laura had gone into the wrong room, but I knew in my heart, it was wishful thinking. It wasn't Laura. My father wasn't coming down that hall either, no matter how much I wanted him to.

"Sondra? Are you still there?"

"I'm here. I thought for a minute I saw Laura but it wasn't her."

"Remember Mom always used to tell us when she threatened to spank us that no one was coming to save us? Remember that? She told us there were no guardian angels and no Jesus, at least not the one that saved children from spankings. She told us we were on our own. There was no Santa and no Easter Bunny, and what we ought to do is give credit where credit was due, be smart, and look out for ourselves. What kind of mother does that?"

"What's your point, Vincent?"

"We have to do this, Sis. No one is coming to save us."

Here was where Vincent usually laughed, but he didn't. I envisioned him sitting on Dad's bed, looking down to the floor at Dad's body.

"I'll tell her that Dad's fallen and you've called 911. That's close to the truth, close enough anyway. I can tell her that." In this case, close enough would have to do.

"That doesn't solve the problem, Sondra. What if they want to take him to a funeral home? What am I going to tell them? I guess I can tell them to take him to the morgue until we decide what to do." Vincent was the one who could think in these situations. I seemed to be the one who shut down. I didn't like that about myself but there it was.

"I have to go, Vincent. Mom's gotten out of bed."

Mom had gotten up to go to the bathroom and I could hear her in there, coughing and wheezing at the effort it took her to make the trip. There was a depression where patient after patient had laid in the spot my mother had just vacated, where she'd pushed blankets nearly off the bed. I was standing in the doorway of her private room when the woman from palliative care returned.

I took her by the elbow and pulled her down the hall a little way. "My father's had an accident," I told her. Why did I do that? Why couldn't I just say it? But I couldn't say it even in my own head. The words wouldn't formulate; my mouth wouldn't let them pass. I thought maybe Vincent was wrong, had made some kind of mistake. To say my father was dead felt like a lie.

"Is it serious? You mean a car accident?" She hugged her clipboard to her chest.

"Can we sit down?" We sat down on one of the couches that lined the corridor. I took a deep breath. "No, not a car accident. My father is eighty-two." I knew this circuitous path in me and I knew I was in danger of telling my father's whole life story as if telling his story would clarify his sudden departure, how he got things done and didn't procrastinate, how he went to college at the age of sixteen and graduated in three years, how he asked my mother to marry him on their second date. He was efficient. Was that going to be on his tombstone? He was efficient? I tried to reel myself in.

"Is he in the hospital?" Her nametag said Mona March and she'd probably dealt with people like me before.

I shook my head no.

"Has your father passed away?" Mona put down her clipboard and reached for my hand.

I nodded my head yes.

"Aww, sweetie." Mona hugged me. "Sometimes this happens. An elderly couple like them…and…well….it's just too much. He probably came to see her every day in this freezing weather." She patted my shoulder. "You haven't told your mother?"

Bless Mona. Sometimes, someone does come to save you. Mother was back in her bed when we went into her room. Mona went to her and straightened the blankets, smoothed them in short, deliberate sweeps of her hand.

"Well?" My mother was almost belligerent. "What's keeping him? What's so god-damned important that he can't show up to get his wife home from the hospital? I'm dying here! He's got better things to do?"

Mona was on one side of the bed and I went to the other. I took my mother's hand. Mona had said that was the thing to do. "Mom, Dad's had an accident."

"Sondra?" Mona urged me on.

"In the car? He crashed into a tree or something? Accident? What kind of accident? He's all right though?" My mother was annoyed and impatient and I wondered how I developed this evasive trait when there was no one to pass it on to me.

"Mom," I had to tell her. She was like a pressure cooker. I had to tell her before she exploded. "Dad didn't make it."

There. I said it.

"Sondra, your dad didn't make what? What are you trying to say?" Mom's hand tightened around mine. She knew. I'm sure she knew but she had to hear me say it. I looked at Mona. She looked directly into my eyes, encouraging me.

"Mom, Dad passed away." My voice faltered but I had to keep talking before Mom interrupted. "When Vincent went to find him, he was lying on the floor next to his bed. He was all dressed and ready to come and then he just…I don't know…he just collapsed, I guess."

My phone started ringing and I knew it must be Vincent. This time, I didn't leave the room to answer it. Mona had pulled a chair closer to Mom's bed; she held Mom's hand and spoke soothingly to her, "Tell me about your husband. How long were you two married?" she cooed.

I had the phone to my ear but I didn't speak.

"Sis? Are you there?"

I nodded, then choked out, "I'm here."

"The paramedics have to take him to the morgue to be declared dead by a doctor, you know, the coroner. And they have to do an autopsy because he died at home with an undetermined cause of death. They have to figure out the cause of death for the gift certificate. Fuck! I mean death certificate. Have you told her?

How's she doing?"

"Are you coming back to the hospital?"

"Don't tell me she died too?"

"No, no, she's sitting here, I think, in shock. It's shocking. We're all in shock."

Mona left again, but before she did, she told me that Mother couldn't go home if there was no one there to look after her. She couldn't live alone. There were alternatives, she said, good places that cared for people with her health problems. I couldn't tell what my mother thought although I studied her face rather than looked at Mona. Mom was trying to focus on what Mona was saying but she wasn't getting any of it, maybe a word here and there, "nursing home," for instance, or "alone" that I imagine rang in her ears and rattled around her head preventing her from absorbing anything more. She'd be back, she told us, when Vincent was here too, oh, and wasn't there another sister?

Mother was asleep when Vincent returned. She had exhausted herself with her overwhelming anxiety, not just that her husband of almost fifty years had died, but that she was stuck in the hospital with no good alternatives. She was in a position in which grieving for my father was, at the same time, grieving for herself. How sweet it would be, she'd said, to die so suddenly, to die without effort, just to be taken from life with perhaps only a second of recognition that this was your end, your last glimpse of light, your last gasp of air. Perhaps a second, perhaps not even that. She resented that she was condemned to lie in bed thinking about her own death while he got off Scott free. I had tried to keep my face neutral when Mona talked about my mother's inability to live alone, tried to give nothing away. I had my own place and Vincent had his place with Carly, his wife, their two-year-old daughter, Sasha, and newborn son, Noah. I could relate to her resentment but I tried not to let it show. Now, Vincent and I were talking about what to do.

"It wouldn't be fair to Carly. She has her hands full and we really don't have room for Mom. We'd have to convert the dining room. How would you feel about moving in with her?"

"It isn't that simple. Moving in with Mom wouldn't be that big a problem, but someone has to be there with her twenty-four hours a day. I'd have to quit my job. I don't want to do that. I shouldn't have to do that. I can't do that. I wouldn't recover financially. Carly doesn't have a job; I could help after work."

We sat there looking down at our feet. We

didn't want to look at Mom or at each other. We were not just avoiding each other, we were avoiding the words nursing home. I felt guilty already and I'm sure Vincent did too. We were avoiding saying that Mom couldn't last a year.

I could see Dr. Patterson coming down the hall. Our lights were dimmed but the hall lights were bright. Dr. Patterson was whistling softly. He swung through the door just as Mom was turning and opening her eyes.

"You all packed up, Elizabeth?"

We filled Dr. Patterson in on the current turn of events. The more we said it, our father died suddenly, the less painful it seemed to be. When the responses were sympathetic but not mortifying, it seemed as though his death wasn't quite so devastating, almost normal. A good long life. Eighty-two years old! An easy death. For him, maybe, but not for us. Each time it was repeated, Mom seemed to struggle with trying to bring that news into reality. I hadn't seen him in death. He was just absent to me; he was just late.

Dr. Patterson was still there when Mona March walked in again carrying a large notebook. In bold, black letters on the front, it said: Extended Care: Palliative, Hospice, and Nursing Facilities. Dr. Patterson took Mom's hand and patted it.

"You take care, Elizabeth," he said.

My mother didn't take part in the conversation with Mona but seemed to be listening intently. Both Vincent and I tried to include her, "Mom, what do you think?" or "Did you hear that, Mom?" but our mother didn't answer. Sometimes she turned her head away and sometimes she said, "What? I didn't catch that." It was as though she were already on her own path to death, angry that our father had beat her to the punch. It was like he'd stolen her shining moment by purposely diverting attention to himself.

"Your father took the easy way," Mom grimaced. She was filled with thoughts of him and nothing more could enter her brain.

Vincent and I were huddled over Mona's notebook looking at pictures of facilities that seemed nice, sun coming through skylights, large community rooms, sparkling dining rooms. With Dad's insurance, social security, and the sale of their house, we could pay for it if she didn't linger too long. She seemed fine and the oxygen tube that would follow her home was hardly noticeable. She was dying of heart failure and lung disease and nothing was going to restore her. She was alive for now and that had to be dealt with. We all looked up from the notebook at the same time like little birds about to be fed.

My mother's expression was one of annoyance. "And we want to be cremated, both of us, and put in the same urn and the urn should be interred at Willow Hill Cemetery. We don't want people looking at our corpses saying how good we look! We're dead for Christ's sake and it isn't a social occasion. We're not turkeys on the Thanksgiving table. We're not display mannequins. Preserving a dead body is like preserving a can after you've dumped out the beans. The beans are gone. The can has no value."

I'd heard this before when our father wanted her to go with him to his mother's funeral. He was a believer in good-byes, last rites, honoring the dead, but Mom was horrified by all that. Honor the living, she'd say, honor life. A corpse is nothing. A corpse is trash. Throw it on a trash heap, but don't lay it in a coffin all dressed in its Sunday best and stuffed with formaldehyde. She thought viewing dead bodies was barbaric and I tended to agree with her. It's Dad's body we're talking about now and hers too. I felt sure she would impose her will on Dad's body as he probably would have on hers.

"Mom, we don't have to think about that right now, at least not for you. I'm glad to know that you and Dad have a plan and that he should be cremated." Vincent was calm and not judgmental, but he was in his teacher mode dealing with a recalcitrant student. "Right now, Mom, we just have to decide what's going to make you the most comfortable, how you can best be taken care of."

"Call Dr. Kevorkian," she said. "Get it over with. I don't want to linger. Who wants to linger? Nobody wants that."

Vincent got up and stood beside her. He put his arm around her shoulders careful not to pull her oxygen tube loose. "We love you, Mom, and we want to keep you with us as long as we can, but we also want you to have the best care and I just don't know if me or Sondra can provide that. I mean, it's going to be difficult for us to bathe you and to make sure we can come when you need us. There are nurses in these facilities and they're set up to handle your care. They're nice places. Take a look." He motioned for me to bring the book over.

"Vinny, what are you afraid of? That you're going to let me die or that you're going to kill me? I don't care. I'm ready."

"But, *we're* not ready." I walked toward them, book in hand. "We just lost our father. We don't want to lose you too." I put the book in front of her but she pushed it away.

"Get out, all of you. I'm a sick old lady whose husband just left her and I need my sleep."

Vincent kissed her and I did the same. Mona pulled Mother's covers up over her shoulders. Then, we went into the hall.

My father hadn't been gone for twenty-four hours but I missed him so much. These kinds of decisions needed his input. He could always handle Mom, calm her jumpy soul and get her to focus. What better hands to leave Mom in than his? Without him…well, we were at a loss.

We had just barely settled into conversation, Mona balancing the notebook in one hand while pointing out features of the residences with the other when Vincent peeked around me and said, "Is she up? What's she doing?" and took off for her room again. Mona and I followed.

"What are you doing, Mom? I thought you were tired. I thought you wanted to sleep. You should have waited for one of us if you needed the bathroom."

Mom didn't answer him but went to the closet and got her clothes. She returned and steadied herself on the side of the bed. Then, off came her hospital gown so quickly that we all dropped our jaws. Muttering under his breath, Vincent left the room. "Oh, my, Mrs. Hendricks!" Mona started moving toward her but stopped, "I'll get Dr. Patterson." Mona's voice drifted behind her as she left the room.

At first I watched my mother fumble. There was no way she was going to get her underwear on. She didn't have the balance to stand on one foot or the agility to bend that low. But I couldn't move. She was so thin, her breasts sagging, her belly extended, her muscles sliding down her body like wax down a burning candle. Finally, I forced myself into motion. I closed her door and went to her. I bent and took hold of her panties. She rested one hand on the bed and the other on my back as she lifted one leg and then the other not more than an inch off the floor. When we'd finished, I opened the door and Vincent came in again.

Mom was wheezing and gasping from the effort when I helped her back into bed.

"Mom, you aren't discharged, you know. You just can't walk out of here."

"Watch me," she said, attempting to get up but falling back into her pillow.

"Wait for Dr. Patterson. Mona's gone to get him and he should be here any minute. Stay put, will you?"

But Mom didn't stay put. She managed to get

up again and out of bed. She hadn't brought a purse but I had left her wallet in the hospital drawer with a little cash and her medical cards. There was a plastic bag; she put her wallet in that along with a toothbrush and a box of tissues. She took the oxygen tube off and laid it on the bed. She wobbled and steadied herself, putting both hands flat on her blankets, her head hanging as if she were about to fall asleep right where she was standing. Vincent rushed to her side.

"Mom, please get in bed. I promise you, if you'll just wait for Dr. Patterson, if you'll just wait to be released, we'll take you anywhere you want to go."

"Where's Alfred?" Mom gripped both of Vincent's forearms to hold herself up. "Where is he? I want to see him."

"Oh, Mom, do you really? Don't you want to remember him as he was?"

"I have a right to say goodbye to my husband, your father. I have that right!"

Her knees buckled then and Vincent picked her up easily and laid her on the bed. I put the oxygen tubes back in place.

When Dr. Patterson came in, Mom was lying on top of her covers, fully dressed, the plastic bag in lieu of purse still over her arm and her hands clasped across her stomach.

"You don't like us anymore?"

"You said I could go home. I'm going home."

"I'm a man of my word. There's no reason you shouldn't go home and you should do that as soon as we have someone there to make sure you're all right. It may take a little while longer, but if that's what you want, Elizabeth, that's what you should have."

Vincent was still standing next to Mom and she grabbed his shirt, "Take me to see Alfred," she pleaded.

Vincent made a few calls. They'd brought his father's body to the hospital that Vincent was calling from, right downstairs. He'd officially been declared dead and was waiting for the autopsy. There was a room for loved ones to say goodbye or sometimes identify bodies and his mother could see her husband there. "Give us a few minutes," the orderly told him, "and I'll freshen him up and wheel him into the viewing area."

Mona got a wheel chair for Mother and packed her oxygen tank in the back of it.

"Do I look alright?" she asked us. "I don't think anybody's combed my hair since I got here."

"You look fine, Mom," Vincent told her, but I took out my comb and lipstick. I pinched a little lipstick on her cheeks too.

"Better? I'm going to the morgue; I don't want to be mistaken for a corpse."

It was a shock to see our usually animated Dad so still. He had been the strong one who was going to live, as Mom always said, forever. I expected him to reach out his hand for Mom, to tell her that everything was going to be okay. And, Mom, who professed not to value the body, as if it were like the rind of an orange to be tossed out, smoothed the sheet that covered him.

"I knew you'd leave me one day, you son of a bitch."

Tears were streaming down my face and down Vincent's too, but Mom was dry-eyed.

"Just when I need you the most, you crap out on me. I'm going home you know. With you or without you, I'm going home. And, I'm going to live forever!"

I guess we were taking her home. I guess we were going to stay with her for a couple of days until we figured things out. I guess I could take bereavement leave until things were settled. I made an appointment for Mona to come to the house and tell us what the options were.

Dad would go from here to the crematorium and, when we picked up his ashes, they would give us the death certificate. It seemed too simple. Simple but not easy, as Dad used to say.

We went back up to Mom's room where she would sign the release forms, and we would gather her half-used paraphernalia of boxes of tissues, creams, non-slip socks. I put them in her bag and Vincent pulled the car around. When we saw Vincent's car at the door, the nurse wheeled Mom out. I sensed Laura's presence and I turned to look in the corners of the building. There she was in her tattered coat and men's boots. She saw me, she waved her hand in front of her face shaking her head, no, shhh, she mouthed. I opened the car door for Mom and tucked her inside and shut her door; I got in my car to follow them. Then, I turned around. I needed to go back and talk to Laura. Someone needed to tell her that our father was dead.

By the time I got there, though, the corner was empty. She couldn't have gone far so I cruised slowly, looking off the main routes of the sidewalk into the lawns. She had gotten two blocks before I caught up with her. I honked and motioned to her but she didn't notice or she was used to being honked at — I don't know. I pulled over and parked a little ahead of her and asked her to come sit in the warm car with me.

The news that our father died didn't seem to faze her. She seemed to have a brief moment of confusion as though what I'd said made no sense. I guess it didn't. Okay, he wasn't in the prime of his life but he was strong and healthy for his age — at least, he seemed to be strong and healthy. She sat there quietly, breathing evenly and freely and the confused face melted away.

"He's gone?" she said.

I nodded. "Forever."

"And Mom? How is she?"

We exchanged a few words and I asked her if she was hungry or if she'd like to take a shower, come and see Mom. To my surprise, she agreed.

"Dad died?" she asked again. I assured her that he had.

Mom was asleep when Laura and I got home. Vincent had settled her in Laura's old room, unable to face the room where our father had died. Laura decided to take a bath while Vincent made some sandwiches. Laura's bath was so long that I went to check on her thinking that she might have just walked out the door again. But she had fallen asleep in the tub, the water gone cold, the bubbles slowly disappearing. When I woke her and told her Mom was still asleep but that Vincent had made some sandwiches, she rinsed and dried herself, wrapped her wet hair in a towel and put on one of Mom's bathrobes. She looked almost like my sister when she sat down at the table.

Vincent started explaining that we had to find a place to put Mom, someplace where she'd be taken care of.

"I'm here now," Laura said between bites, not looking up, being her quiet self. "I'm here," she repeated.

Vincent and I looked at each other. Laura had been on the streets for decades, in and out of mental facilities and drug rehab. She'd graduated to homeless shelters, then, more or less disappearing. We couldn't trust her to be Mom's caretaker but neither of us knew what to say.

Vincent tried to be diplomatic, "But what about you? What about your life?"

Laura just shrugged. "Is there another sandwich?"

I made Laura another sandwich and put it on her plate. "Laura, have you been taking your medication? Are you sober?"

"I'll take care of her," Laura said, this time looking me straight in the eye, not asking permission, challenging.

"What does a girl have to do to get some service in here?" Mom yelled from the bedroom.

"I guess Mom's awake," Vincent said getting up.

Laura wiped her hands on the napkin in her lap.

"You can trust me, you know," she said, very direct, looking at me without flinching. "I lied to you yesterday; I'm sure you knew it. I stay in a shelter when I can get a bed and when I can't I know where some garages are unlocked. Mom leaves the garage unlocked for me. She put a cot in there behind all the boxes and old furniture so Dad wouldn't see it. Sometimes she leaves money, a few dollars for some food. I never take it...well, sometimes. I want to make it look like I was never there. But I'm different now. You can trust me. I want to take care of Mom. Please let me."

I was speechless. Laura took a few more bites, wiped her mouth, and got up. "I better go talk to her," she said.

Vincent passed Laura in the hall, looked at her then at me raising his eyebrows.

We heard a little cry from Mom when Laura crossed her threshold and then nothing. I really wanted to sneak a peek but more than that I wanted them to have their private moment. All of a sudden I was crying, sobbing uncontrollably. Vincent was making a cup of tea for Mom. "It's okay, Sis," he said. "It's going to be okay." I could imagine him talking to his toddler that way as he prepared lunch to set on the tray of the high chair. I blew my nose in my napkin but fell into sobbing again. Vincent didn't take the tea in when it was ready but sat across from me at the table.

"What do you think we ought to do?" he asked.

I sniffled, tried to catch my breath, "About what? Dad? Mom? Laura?"

"Yes," he said.

"I don't know. Maybe we ought to give Laura a chance. What's the worst that can happen?" Was I being self-serving? I didn't know.

"Well, she could leave Mom to suffer for starters. She could walk out and not feed her and not make sure she gets to the bathroom. She could sell Mom's meds on the street, sell her furniture, empty her bank account. Can Laura even drive?" Vincent was frustrated but not angry.

"I'm not saying we ought to give her free reign," I told him. "One of us has to come every day and call too and talk to Mom, not Laura. We have to monitor her care. Wouldn't we do that anyway?"

Vincent nodded. "I suppose. Maybe we could hire a nurse or a housekeeper too. Someone to keep an eye on Mom and on Laura."

Vincent got up to take Mom's tea in and I followed behind him. We could hear soft murmuring coming from Laura's room. There they were; my sister had gotten under the covers with Mom. She was sitting up leaning against the headboard with a sheaf of paper in her hand. Mom was lying down facing away from her daughter, her head on her pillow.

"Come in, children," Mom whispered, not opening her eyes and not raising her head. "Laura is reading to us."

Vincent set the tea on the bedside table and took a seat on the floor. I sat on Laura's baby blue velvet slipper chair. I wanted my sister home, clean and sober, and there she sat wrapped in Mom's white terry cloth robe, her freshly-washed hair turbaned in a towel. I settled back and pushed my shoes off with my toes. While our mother was in the hospital, I brought in her mail and piled it on the nightstand. The papers in Laura's hands were Mom's junk mail. Laura was reading a sales letter from a vacation realtor telling Mom that she'd won a trip to St. Petersburg, Florida; her only obligation was attendance at a presentation.

"Save that," our mother mumbled, "We may want to go there."

After a while, Vincent got up, stretched, kissed his sleeping mother and his two sisters, and left. With Mom sleeping soundly, Laura and I went into the kitchen.

"The telephone numbers are here," I told her pointing to the list taped to the side of the refrigerator. "There's plenty of food, Mom kept the freezer full, but if you need something, call me. If Mom takes a turn for the worst, call me."

"You were always a worrier, Sondra. Don't worry so much! We'll be fine."

I can't say panic didn't set in as soon as Laura shut the door behind me, or that it wasn't already on my mind to call in a few hours. I glanced back at the house where I grew up and saw that Laura had turned on the living room lights and the windows were golden as if a happy family lived there. And we were a happy family even though our father just died and our mother was soon to follow, even though our parents valued a writer's words over their children's or even their own words.

I knew what Mom would say, of course. She'd say, as if it were all so self-evident, "What value are words, after all, spoken out and evaporating into the air? Better that the words be materialized, fastened to the world on a page so that they can be examined, revisited like court records, like evidence. What good are words manifested only in our breath? They are as transient as smoke signals."

I looked up to see Laura standing at the window. She waved as I drove away.

Statues in a Blue Garden

Georgette Landau often lies in bed and imagines that she is growing younger, that her white hair is returning to the lustrous auburn it once was and that her skin is taking on the glow of youth. She imagines a lithe body, alive with energy; she imagines small but buoyant breasts ready for a young man's touch. She looks at the baroque ceiling of her ancient house, not smiling, simply waiting for her transformation to youth to complete itself. She knows, in reality, when she rises, the aches and stiffness that are the rewards of her age will overtake her. She admonishes herself that it is unwise to be at the end of life's path with dreams that are neither realized nor forsaken and with a heart that is neither healed nor broken…a condition for a young girl. Surely, she muses, life ends with satisfactory resolutions, with the neat disposition of ambitions that are ticked off as achieved or dismissed, with love that is unquestionably won or lost. Surely, Georgette thinks, no grey areas will remain when she is laid to rest.

A timid rap and the door opens ushering in Lucy carrying Georgette's breakfast tray. "Madam," she greets her, "you are well this morning?" Lucy came to her as a teenager and Georgette had schooled her in English, which she speaks with a heavy accent.

Georgette sweeps aside her rose-colored, satin comforter and gets up. "Put the tray on the desk, please, Lucy." The servant obeys and asks if Madam would like the shades open so that she can see her beautiful garden in the golden light of the Parisian morning. Lucy is already at it, so Georgette doesn't bother to answer.

"Will you start a bath for me, please?"

"Lavender or Gardenia, Madam?"

"I think Lavender." Georgette looks out the window into her hydrangea garden, a sea of blue in the temperate Parisian soil. The tables are already placed and the workmen are just setting out the chairs. Nancy is cutting hydrangea blooms to put in vases for the tables. Opening the window and leaning out, Georgette musters her most commanding voice, "Nancy! Nancy! Cut the ones facing the street, not the ones that will face our guests! The garden should look full and lush, painted with blue blooms! Don't leave just the greenery to see!"

Nancy moves without comment to the other side of the hydrangea bushes, snugging herself between the wall that protects the house from the street and the overgrown bushes.

"What's the time?" Georgette asks Lucy.

"Just nine-thirty, Madam."

"And when are we expecting guests?"

"Eleven-thirty."

"Are we using the white china? I want to use the ones with the peacocks on them. Are they being readied?"

"Let me help you into your bath and then I'll check. I believe that, yes, Nancy has the peacock plates ready."

Lucy helps Georgette into the tub and, when she is settled, leaves her.

Lavender was Richard's favorite. Oh, that was a long time ago. What does she actually know about him now? They haven't seen each other for almost fifty years; he was twenty-five and she was twenty-two. Of course, she'd heard news of him from time to time, seen his picture in the society pages when he married Marianne Hauptman and in the business pages when he was promoted. Georgette had married too. Life goes on. She had been born Georgia Newhouse and married Herbert Landau, a man she called Bertie. Bertie's mother was French and his father had been a one star general stationed in Europe. His father was often absent but, because he loved his wife and wanted to please her, allowed her to stay in Paris while he alternated between Paris, Germany, Washington, sometimes even Japan or Korea. Herbert Landau, Bertie, was raised in America and France. He was bilingual so when his firm, an international law firm, decided to open a branch in Paris, Bertie was a shoe-in. Five years after their marriage, he was assigned to the Paris office and they were happier there than even these perpetual newlyweds ever could have imagined. Two years later, over wine in a favorite restaurant with a view of the Seine and the Notre Dame, they'd decided it was time to begin a family. Their apartment was small but comfortable, certainly big enough to add an infant. Bertie thought they would have two years from that day to find a bigger place.

Not long after that dinner on the Seine across from the Notre Dame, Bertie fell ill. It was the flu, they thought, or a virus perhaps, but when he didn't recover in three days, Georgette took Bertie to the hospital. The doctors tried massive infusions of antibiotics but Bertie didn't respond to the treatment. After another three days, Bertie suffered cardiac arrest and didn't recover. He had died at the age of thirty-three and Georgette was left a young widow of twenty-eight.

Yes, she had been happier in Paris than at any time in her life and now she was sadder there too. She took Bertie's body home to Boston to be buried in his family's plot that, at the time, was occupied only by his grandparents. She knew she'd have to return to Paris, have to dismantle the apartment, have to ship things home to her parents at least for the time being. Without Bertie, she couldn't afford the Marais apartment but once inside the cool plaster walls of the apartment they had shared, she knew she couldn't abandon it. She could neither stay nor go. Her landlord was generous, but after the third month of unpaid rent, he apologetically served her with an eviction notice. Still, she sat glumly in her apartment, the lights off, rocking in her chair in the dark.

Then, tragedy struck again. Three months after Bertie's death, to cope with their grief over the loss of their only son, his parents, very wealthy by anyone's standards, decided a cruise would be just the thing to lift their sorrow an inch. Off the coast of Italy, though, their ship rammed a huge boulder. The captain, unwilling to admit even to himself that he had made an error, thought the ship had no more than run aground due to faulty maps and ordered passengers to remain in their staterooms. It wasn't a simple miscalculation that sent the ship into shallow waters merely stranding them; the boulder had ripped a massive cavity in the ship's hull and water was rushing in faster than the passengers could flee. Bertie's parents were swept out to sea and their bodies never found. Their will, of course, left everything to their only son Herbert. There had been no thought or time to change it and the courts, also by an act of generosity and lack of contention, awarded the fortune to Georgette Landau, previously Georgia Newhouse. She bought the house she now lived in, and she remained unmarried and childless. Over time, she became Georgette instead of Georgia to diminish the distance between her and France the country she loved from the first time she set eyes on it. She understood that a life demands a certain vocabulary—not just the jargon of one's trade, in her case the widow's trade—but a vocabulary that expressed who she was, what she thought, her joys and sorrows. She was no longer Georgia Newhouse. She was Georgette Landau and her vocabulary was French and full of hope and sorrow.

Besides the Landau fortune, Bertie's company had paid out life insurance money to her and offered her investment advice. With inherited money and the insurance settlement, Georgette had lived comfortably all these years.

And now Richard Cummings had written her a letter. She had loved only two men in her entire life: one was her husband, Bertie Landau, and the other was Richard Cummings.

Richard had known her only as Georgia Newhouse, a pert blonde in the steno pool at Hitchens and Hitchens, a small firm that manufactured custom boxes for high-end department stores. Richard, the ink still wet on his business degree, had landed a management position at the company. He and Georgia often found themselves in the elevator together, not alone, but with other young women from the steno pool, all of whom thought Mr. Cummings a dreamboat supreme and teased her mercilessly when he asked her out to dinner.

It was nineteen-fifty-three. Richard was her first romance. She felt that her dreams had come true and, as soon as the ring was on her finger, they would consummate their love in an extraordinary and thrilling night when the moon was full and the stars twinkled in the sky. As it happened, consummation did not depend on a ring but on the stirring of passion in a secluded wood. There, Georgia Newhouse shed the blood that ties a woman to a man.

"Madam?" Lucy's face shows at the edge of the door. "May I help you out?"

"That would be nice; yes."

Lucy takes the bath sheet from a heated towel rack and wraps it gently around Georgette as she steps gingerly out of the tub. There was talk of installing a roll-in shower, roll-in for those using a wheelchair, everything non-slip, everything made of pliable rubber, no hard surfaces. "Not yet!" Georgette laughed. "I'm not ready for that yet!" But as she lifts her leg over the edge of the deep tub and feels the foot still in the tub slip a little, she panics and grabs Lucy around the waist.

"I've got you, Madam," Lucy says, clutching Georgette with her towel-covered arms. "You won't fall. I've got you."

Lucy pats Georgette with the towel and then uses a puff to powder her dry. She helps her with her slippers and robe and sits her in front of her dressing table.

"Shall I re-heat your breakfast?"

"No, thank you. It doesn't matter," she says lifting the tepid tea to her lips.

Georgette hastily organized a garden party when she got Richard's letter. She didn't want to see him for the first time in so many years without the support of her friends. There would be twelve in all, gathered around three tables in her blue hydrangea garden.

"What time is it, Lucy?" Georgette asks.

"Ten-thirty, Madam."

One hour, thinks Georgette. Does she feel dread? Fear? Anticipation? She can't name it. It isn't butterflies in her stomach or heart-stopping anxiety; it isn't like being wheeled down a corridor into an operating room or opening doors behind which a ruined surprise party waits. It's different from anything she's ever felt. It's like loss in a way and at the same time also like a gift. Maybe it's like a wedding day when a young bride faces the unknown, so much depending on the love of a man. Yes, that's it. That's what she was feeling…on the edge of something.

Georgette dresses slowly and deliberately, a chiffon dress she loves but has, nonetheless, hung in the closet unworn for years.

"How does this look, Lucy?"

"Lovely, Madam."

Lucy can't be trusted to tell her the truth.

"You don't think it's too youthful? Look how my skin sags at the neck. No, this dress won't do. Get rid of it!" Georgette tosses the dress on her bed.

Nancy knocks softly at the door and lets herself in. "Madam, there's a man at the door. His name is Richard Cummings. Shall I let him in?"

He's early! Has he no manners? Georgette is not yet presentable. Still, she can't let him wander the streets.

"Take him into the garden and offer him tea. Oh, he's American. Offer him coffee even at this hour. Tell him I'll be down soon."

Georgette looks out the window until she sees Richard appear accompanied by Nancy. From her second floor window Georgette can only discern the obvious: he is heavier, a little slump-shouldered, his hair grey and sparse. A panama hat rests in his hands; his white linen suit is impeccable. He walks in and sits down with the grace of a younger man. A minute later, a waiter hired for the day brings him coffee, a little cup on a big silver tray.

Georgette fusses as Lucy combs her hair. "Oh, I should have asked Mimi for a tint—my hair is so dull! This dress is ridiculous. What else is in the closet?" And again, "What time is it, Lucy?"

"Eleven-fifteen, Madam."

She's kept him waiting for fifteen minutes. Serves him right for coming early. She changes into the lavender and then into the blue dress the color of the flowers in the garden. No, she would look like one big hydrangea. She changes into a white chiffon that she often wears for lunch. She likes its lightness, its flow, cloud-like she thinks. The high lace Victorian collar of the dress fits snugly around her neck almost to her jaw line. Her hair is swept up in a French twist as it was the last time she saw him. This time, though, wisps of white hair escape giving her a glowing aura around her ivory face.

"I think this is the best we can do," Georgette sighs.

She looks out her window. The garden chair where Richard was sitting is now empty, his cup abandoned on the table. He's gone. She has kept him waiting too long and now he's gone. But then, she sees the top of the Panama hat he carried and maybe even the tip of his spectator shoes and she realizes he is only looking at the ornamentation of the house. She isn't going to take the chance that he will wander away before she's had a chance to see him up close, before she has a chance to ask what happened, what it was that took him away from his job never to return. She'd asked other girls in the steno pool and no one seemed to know. The handsome Mr. Cummings had simply vanished.

Georgette descends the stairs slowed by trepidation and by the heaviness of the by-gone years. She toys with putting a bounce in her step but feels too silly, as though she is perpetrating a kind of hoax. She rounds the corner at the bottom of the stairs and goes into the kitchen to look out the window at Richard who is still alone in the garden.

"What time is it, Lucy?" she asks.

"Twenty-past, Madam. Shall I bring your tea into the garden?"

Georgette pivots thinking she should not enter the garden through the kitchen but through the French doors leading out from the salon. Richard's back is to her; she's glad she has a chance just to look at him for a moment. She opens the door. He doesn't turn. He hums softly, his hands in his pockets.

"Richard." There is relief in her voice. Richard doesn't turn.

The garden gate opens and in floods her guests, all of them in one fell swoop, chattering as they probably had walking down the street to her house. Georgette turns toward the new arrivals, smiling, just as Richard turns toward her. She walks toward the arriving guests extending both hands toward them, welcoming them, an air kiss on each cheek.

The moment slipped away. They missed their chance to come face to face in the quiet of the blue garden. When Richard's eyes finally meet Georgette's, Georgette is leading a gaggle of guests in his direction. She holds the hand of one of her friends and extends the other to Richard.

"Richard?" she says as though she isn't quite sure and yet she is sure. She is very, very sure. His face is older, no question, even his eyes have aged, not as open, not as bright, and his smile has a kind of dullness about it. He stands a bit awkwardly saying nothing, looking at her in a vacant sort of way.

"How are you, my old friend?" When Richard doesn't extend his hand, she clutches his arm just above the elbow. "Richard, this is my best friend,

Anna. Anna, this is my old friend, Richard Cummings."

Richard stirs, then smiles. "Nice to meet you," he says. Georgette continues to introduce her friends. Richard shakes hand after hand, smiling quietly, nodding nervously.

The hired man is just bringing out tea. The weather, while there is no chill, is pleasantly cool. Some of the ladies wear light shawls and the men wear summer jackets. The tea is poured and distributed. Cakes and sandwiches are brought out on tiered platters. The peacock china is stacked neatly on the blue linen tablecloth. The obligations of the hostess complete, Georgette now wants Richard to herself.

"Let's sit down, Richard. Over there." Georgette takes Richard's arm and leads him to a place at the table, motioning Nancy to bring him a cup of tea.

He doesn't look at her and Georgette fights back feelings of confusion and anger. He starts to hum again; Georgette puts her hand on his knee.

"Richard, have you come to Paris alone? All on your own?" she asks.

"Come alone? Yes. Well, no, I have a driver. Nice fellow." Richard looks around, watching the door, watching the gate. "He'll wait for me."

Georgette is at a loss. This doesn't match the scenario she constructed in her head ever since the letter came. Why had he come? What had he come to say?

"Would you like some milk? Or sugar? Can I get you a sandwich?" She wanted to take hold of both his ears and turn his face to hers.

"Do you know the time? I've come to see a friend and she seems to be late."

"A friend?"

"Yes. Her name is Georgia Newhouse. You must know her. She should be here by now. I met her years ago. She was in the steno pool where I worked. Beautiful. She was beautiful."

Georgette's shoulders fall, her head sags down, her arms go limp but only for a second. It is clear that his mind is more than waning. She recovers herself.

"Were you in love with her?" Georgette can't keep herself from asking.

"If she doesn't come soon, my driver will leave without me. You know the French…no tolerance for Americans."

"I'm sure he'll wait for you, Richard. Don't be anxious about that. I'll ask Lucy to take him some tea."

"You're so kind. You must be Georgia's

grandmother, yes?"

Georgette is aware that her friends are slyly peeking and whispering about the old beau she talked so much about, how she was looking forward to this day, had invited a group of friends out of joy and apprehension. Anna was so happy for her, so many years had gone by alone; new hope sprung up that Georgette might avoid spending her last days rattling around her big, empty house with just her servants for companionship.

As is Georgette's way, she laughs a little at the thought that she could be Georgia Newhouse's grandmother and thinks for a brief second that she might tell him that, yes, that's exactly who she is. She wanted to say, what happened to you, Richard? Why did you leave me so suddenly and without a word? We were all so confused! I waited, Richard, and then I saw.... Georgette thought of the engagement announcement. After all these years, there was still a twinge of pain. She thought only this morning that life should end with everything all sorted out, no loose ends, no unresolved relationships, no unresolved angers, all mysteries solved. There is nothing to do but let go, to forgive what couldn't be explained or known, what he could not remember, let alone communicate to her.

"Where did the two of you meet?" Georgette asks instead.

"She didn't tell you?" He tilts his head closer and whispers, "I think she loves me. I'll scold her for not telling you all about me." Richard straightens, takes a sip from the thin china cup. "We would be in an elevator, the two of us, alone in the company where we both worked. Standing that close to her, I felt heat pouring off her body, such a sweet little body!" He smiles a wistful smile and looks past Georgette into the hydrangeas.

"And when was that? How long ago?"

"Why, it was….maybe…let's see."

Georgette lays her hand over his hoping for some recognition in his eyes.

Richard slips his hand from beneath hers and looks seriously at his own hand as though it were totally alien, that touch had become foreign.

"I must go!" he says suddenly, half-rising from his chair. "My driver won't wait forever!"

"Please stay, Richard. You've come so far to see…" she hesitates, not sure how to go on, but then decides, "…her, Georgia, I mean. Surely you will have a sandwich before you leave or a slice of nice ripe melon? Wait a bit longer, won't you?"

He sits down, his face relaxes again, "Yes, a

sandwich."

Georgette is afraid to leave his side so signals Lucy and soon one of the tiered trays is setting in front of them.

Every line of inquiry Georgette opens seems to cause Richard confusion. She asks about his family, about is wife, and Richard mumbles, expresses concern that his driver will leave him. He opens his wallet, though, and shows her a picture of him and Georgia taken in a booth at an amusement park many decades ago.

"And who is this?" Georgette points to the picture of a child, a school picture, but Richard can't remember. He tells her that sometimes people slip pictures into his wallet without his permission, confusing him.

By one-thirty, the sandwich trays sit barren on the table and her friends begin to drift out, saying briefly that they will talk to her soon and telling Richard how pleased they are to have met him although he talked to no one and they all had kept a discrete distance to let the two of them engage in intimate conversation, each of them wondering if love's flame would spark anew.

As Lucy, Nancy, and the hired man begin to clear the tables, Georgette and Richard walk along the hydrangeas. In the thick of them, Georgette had placed two aubergine Adirondack chairs that face the abundant blooms.

"Richard, I'm so glad you came, but I'm afraid I have sad news." Georgette is unsure if she is doing the right thing. "Georgia Newhouse died a long time ago. She was only twenty-eight. It was me who responded to your recent letter. I'm so sorry for the deceit."

Richard has no reaction. Then, he holds out his hand and Georgette takes it. He says, "Yes, I think her friend Richard died too."

They sit hand in hand until Richard's son walks through the still open gate and heads toward them, their backs to him.

"I'm here for my father," he says to Lucy who is gathering the linen. "Do you think it's okay to interrupt them?"

Lucy nods, not looking up from her task.

Richard's son, a big smile on his face and a confident stride, rounds the chairs and stands before them, the blue wall of hydrangea's behind him.

"You must be Georgia," he says when he faces them. He extends his hand.

She stands, seeing the resemblance immediately.

"Oui, je suis Georgette." She doesn't know

why she suddenly decides to switch to French. It feels like she's reclaiming her own life in some way, coming back to the present. She offers him the tips of her fingers.

"I'm Devin, Dad's oldest." This face, this name, he is the product of the years they had not spent together. "Since my mother died a year ago, Dad thinks of you often," he says looking sadly at his father. "Dad?" Richard is slumped in his chair asleep. "I'm so embarrassed for him," Devin chuckles. "Dad?" He shakes his father's shoulder until Richard rouses. "It's time to go, Dad."

Georgette carries Richard's hat to the gate while Devin holds his father's arm. It is as though Richard were sleepwalking. He says nothing more, too tired, too lost to bid her good-bye.

"I'm not sure Dad will even remember being here. I thought it was a good idea—he mentions you so often." Devin shakes his head sadly. "I thought it might cheer him up."

Georgette stands by the gate until Richard is safely tucked into the car and waves as they drive away; then, she returns to the chair where she sat across from Richard.

She doesn't notice Lucy until she hears her say, "Is there anything I can get you, Madam?"

Georgette shakes her head, no, nothing.

She had been silly, thinking at her age there was a new chapter to open, love yet to be found, or even that life ended in peaceful resolution of all its mysteries. She had longed for an explanation, ignoring the obvious…that Richard had forsaken her for the wealthier, more beautiful Marianne and that Richard had gone to work at Marianne's father's company. It wasn't so much of a mystery really. But Richard hadn't forgotten the young Georgia. It had only gotten too late.

Georgette wasn't aware that Anna had returned until she sat down in the chair across from her. Anna said nothing but reached out for Georgette's hand, which Georgette gladly gave her.

Johnsonville

We decided early on not to stop but to drive straight through to Tacoma to the prison. Elvis had sent a little money, two hundred dollars...not enough for a decent motel, just barely enough for gas really. Two hundred dollars wouldn't buy gas and a place safe enough to leave the car unattended while we slept. My wedding dress was in the backseat and leaving it, even in a locked car, made me nervous. Right now, just about everything made me nervous. Wedding jitters. Normal. Along with the money came instructions to pick up his sister to stand as his best man or my bridesmaid or whatever. We needed family and Shelly was it. So, I had driven into Los Angeles from Encino and there she was, standing on the corner of Tenth and Broadway with a plastic grocery sack, smoking restlessly, meaner-looking than I'd hoped, skinny. She was looking into the street as though she might cross. When she saw the car pulling over, she flicked away her cigarette and got in.

    We'd never met so we looked at each other for a minute until I said, "You're Shelly, right?" and she smiled and buckled her seat belt. It was awkward. I didn't really know what to say. She scared me a little. Her teeth were bad and her skin pocked; her hair was as thin and colorless as rice noodles. She looked like white trash and I didn't want her to be white trash. But what did I expect? I knew she'd been incarcerated too. It was like prison was in her genes, some kind of biological destiny, a salmon swimming up-stream. From the look of her, it had to be drugs, prostitution, or both. She wasn't big enough for assault, although she'd probably given it her best shot more than once. I didn't know what she'd been in for, what her transgressions were, and prison records weren't fodder for casual conversation, at least not where I come from. Maybe she wasn't mean so much as she was rode hard and put away wet, as

Elvis would say. She had some miles on her, for sure, some hard miles. At the very least, though, she was scrappy. I wouldn't want to mess with her.

Why she hadn't been to see Elvis didn't come up either. He'd been in prison more than six years. Maybe she'd been in jail all that time too. I don't know. And, with no money and no car, I guess it would be pretty tough to get from Los Angeles to McNeill Island in Puget Sound. Our conversation in the car seemed pretty normal, not a kindergarten teacher getting to know an offender, but a bride getting to know her future sister-in-law.

"Once," I answered Shelly when she asked if I'd been married before. For the past six hours, we'd talked; the more miles we covered, the more personal the questions got and the longer the answers. Still, it seemed like she was interviewing me — she asked the questions mainly and I tried to give her answers that made sense.

"So? What happened?" Shelly had unzipped her skin-tight jeans and tossed her cowboy boots in the back seat long before we got to San Francisco. We already covered how I met Elvis through the prison pen-pal network and how I visited him after we'd been "dating" for a year.

There were forces at work, our driving through what was now the dark night, our impending lifelong relationship, that made things a little surreal. It felt like a scene in a movie. I needed to focus on the road but every once in a while, I just had to look at her.

"Kathy? What happened?" Shelly persisted.

"I dunno," I shrugged. "Just grew apart I guess."

We'd started out late. I hadn't gassed up before I picked her up, so when we stopped, we each got a hot dog and soda. Now, my stomach was beginning to rumble.

"How long you married?" Shelly was slouched down in the passenger seat with her feet on the dashboard. She lost her driver's license because of multiple D.U.Is, and now I was stuck with driving the whole way. I guess I wouldn't have it any other way.

"Well, officially a year, but we stopped living together after two months."

"You 'grew apart' in two months?" I felt her eyes go wide in the dark.

"It wasn't right from the beginning. I don't really know why I married him."

"You didn't love him? How old were you guys?"

Love? I shrugged, thinking. Surely, it wasn't possible to shock Shelly. No doubt she'd heard everything that she hadn't experienced first-hand. But maybe the failure of a normal marriage between two college graduates with bright futures seemed freakish somehow. If that kind of marriage didn't work...well. I kept my eyes on the road.

"And you guys were how old?" she asked again.

"I was twenty-four and he was twenty-seven." Opportunities to tell this part of my story were rare. My family didn't bring it up and neither did my friends. I had simply left my marriage and went back home to the same room that I had in high school with pictures of Tim Hawkins and me in our prom clothes still tucked in the mirror of my dressing table.

"Let me get this straight. You guys graduate from high school, go to college, get good jobs, and then stay married for two months?"

Shelly lit up a cigarette and cracked her window a little. It was almost Christmas and the farther north we drove the colder it got. The open window felt good, though. I took off a few days early from school so Elvis and I could get married at Christmas. Kindergarteners at Christmas are pretty much a nightmare and, truth be told, I'd rather spend that time at the prison.

Shelly blew smoke toward the open window. "I'm serious, Kathy. That is seriously fucked up. I mean, you should be raising kids and living in the suburbs. Instead, you're driving to god-knows-where to marry a guy in prison for twenty to life? Think, Kathy, think! That is seriously fucked up."

This wasn't news. I heard the same sentiment over and over from my parents, my sister, my friends…from anyone who knew I was engaged to a man who would likely spend his life in prison. And, it wasn't just that he was in prison; he was a man who'd done what he had done, the robbery, the killing he'd never intended, the three-state chase. They couldn't get beyond those facts to see the facts I saw, a repentant man who'd never had a chance in life.

Shelly asked me if I had loved my first husband; after almost a decade, I still couldn't answer that question. I honestly didn't know. Love? It just seemed like love was such a small part of that whole ball of wax.

"There's a time when you have to stop and ask yourself what the hell you're doing," I said to Shelly, glancing at her, at the road, at her again. "Your friends say you're crazy, your mother cries every time she looks at you, your little sister begs you not to do it, your father tries to bribe you, and somehow, you buy the dress, and get in the car and drive twelve hundred miles to get married. But, to tell the truth, I have less doubt about marrying Elvis than I had when I married Mark. He was good looking; you know the type. He had potential. He was a nice guy. I mean, Mark was a truly good man."

"And the problem was?"

"The problem. Yes, well…," I hesitated. How to explain? "I could see my whole life like a pathetic story everybody already knew: really cute kids, soccer, PTA, promotion, house, bigger house."

Shelly's eyebrows go up. "Yeah? And? I don't get it."

"It just made me crazy. I remember exactly when I snapped. Picture this: I'm standing at the kitchen counter making a salad, slicing tomatoes with a paring knife and Mark comes up behind me and puts his arms around me. Well, I just wanted to take that knife and run it right through him." I kept my eyes on the road now. It made me mad all over again remembering. "He's got his cheek against my cheek and it's all I could do not to lift my arm and give him one good thrust right in the eye."

When I finally glanced at Shelly, she was staring at me. She'd stopped mid-chomp on her gum and now her mouth just hung open. I could almost hear her thinking that maybe I should be in jail too and how could anyone in their right mind think that I could be safe teaching kindergarteners anything at all. Well, no, maybe she wasn't thinking that. Shelly was inscrutable.

"I didn't, of course," I assured her. "Instead, I giggled a little and told Mark to let go. When he did, I picked up my purse, walked out the door, and didn't look back. I guess the truth is that a good man like Mark didn't suit me. I mean, if the response to goodness were love, then Anna would have loved Karenin. She didn't. She loved Vronsky."

Shelly gave me a puzzled look that morphed into a smile.

"Shelly, I love Elvis. You can see why. Don't you love your brother?" I took my eyes off the road again and looked at her for what seemed like a long time. I wanted to stare, to leave my eyes on her until I understood her, but that would take a while, that would have to come later, if it ever came at all.

"What kind of shit question is that?" Shelly

stomped the dash with both feet. I was glad she'd taken off her boots. "Hell, no! He beat the hell out of me every day of my life." She took a breath, "No, I take that back; he beat the hell out of me after Dad left. Elvis carried on the tradition." She lit a cigarette off the one she'd just finished and threw the butt into the dark night. "I don't mean it. Elvis, was a troubled kid; I know that." I was amazed at how quickly her anger transformed into pity. "At least Dad wore himself out on Elvis. By the time the old man came after me, he was pretty tired. Gotta love a brother just for that."

"Where was your mom?"

"Tryin' to hide most of the time. She'd crawl under the kitchen table, hug her knees, put her head down. It was like a goddamn air raid. She got a knife after him once, but she lost her nerve. She could have done some damage, but he got the knife and almost cut her ear off. I gotta say, though, there was a bond between those two, my mom and dad."

Shelly sounded almost wistful. I glanced at her love-despite-everything half-smile and swerved to miss coyote road kill.

Shelly rummaged through her purse and came up with a fresh stick of gum. Through her chews she said, "You gettin' hungry? My stomach's growlin'."

It wasn't that Elvis hadn't told me all this, but it's different coming from a woman sitting next to me in my car, a woman I couldn't imagine ever being in my car under any other circumstances.

"Yeah, I'm hungry too. What's next on the map?"

Shelly turned on the overhead light. "Johnsonville. Another eight miles. Crap. Do you think there's anything in Johnsonville?"

"We'll find out."

Johnsonville turned out to be three blocks long with a honky-tonk bar at the end of each block. We picked the one with the most trucks parked in front. The locals always know who has the best food. Shelly pulled down the visor and looked in the mirror, fluffed her lank hair, put on some lipstick. She zipped her jeans and tugged on her boots. I opened the trunk of the car, put on my white satin heels and snugged my wedding veil down tight on my head.

The wedding would be in the room where condemned prisoners meet with their loved ones for the last time. Under the circumstances, it seemed fitting that my bachelorette party/rehearsal dinner should be in a bar in Johnsonville.

"Come on, Sister," I said putting an arm around her shoulder.

"You think you're gonna get lucky dressed like that?" Shelly grinned.

"I'm already lucky," I winked.

Inside, the bar was dark and smoky. Balls broke wildly at three pool tables to our right. Men leaned on cues and watched Shelly and me walk through the door. They smirked at each other, making cracks, no doubt, about my wedding veil. The back of the room was lit up for a three-piece band squeezed onto a small platform. In front of them was a dance floor crowded with couples. On the left side, a bar and stools ran the length of the room from the door to the bandstand. Shelly and I exchanged glances and headed for two vacant bar stools at the end of the bar away from the music. Still, when the bartender came over, we had to yell to be heard.

Before he could speak, I asked if he'd take a credit card.

"Spending the old man's money already?" he grinned. When we didn't smile back, he said, "What can I get you ladies?"

Shelly ordered chicken wings, onion rings, and a beer. I ordered a hamburger with lettuce and tomato and a coke. By the time our order arrived, Shelly had tossed back three frosty glasses of cold beer. We were near the door; often when people left, they called out "Good Luck, Honey" or "Congratulations." I nudged my veil away from Shelly's sauce covered hands.

"How's the burger, bride-girl?" The other bartender had wandered over.

"Don't talk to him, Kathy. That guy looks like he's got the devil on speed dial."

I ignored her. "It's good." I'm not flirting, just responding to an employee inquiring about the quality of the food. "We've been driving for six hours. I think anything would taste good right now." I looked down at my burger and tore off another bite.

"Well, if you ladies need anything, give me a holler," he said taking a swipe at the counter with his bar towel.

"Get me another one, will ya?" Shelly held up an empty glass. Then, the little band began to play "Gettin' You Home" and Shelly slid off her stool and headed for the dance floor. Seeing Shelly out there dancing, caught up in the come-hither tones, her body swaying unselfconsciously, her hands up-lifted making lazy circles in the smoke-filled air, I almost wished I could be more like her. I don't mean an ex-con hooker-junkie, but freer, less guarded, less fearful. It's like she's privileged with some kind of supernatural protection, putting herself out there like an invitation with full confidence that nothing's going to happen to her that she can't handle. I know she's wrong, of course; things happen to women all the time that they don't want to happen, that they aren't prepared to handle, but Shelly seemed oblivious. Her dreamy smile made her look like she'd been kissed by angels. She was enraptured.

Suddenly, I felt this whack, whack, whack on my ass and I thought what the hell? I turned and there's a little jerky farm dude looking sheepish.

"What the hell are you doing!!!??? I haven't been spanked since I was about eight years old; I didn't like it then and I don't like it now."

"I'm sorry, Ma'am," he stammered respectfully. "It's the damn cigarette. Got too close to your bride thingy there and it just went up. Sorry if I had to slap your ass like that, but you were on fire."

I looked down at my veil and sure enough, the entire hem was burned away. It was singed black at the edge fading to smoky brown for another four inches.

"Jess, what have you done, boy?" The bartender, suppressing a smile, came to see what the commotion was about. A few male on-lookers laughed, but the women covered their mouths in horror.

"Didn't mean it, Bud. Sorry, Ma'am. Real sorry." Then he started laughing and I laughed too, a little too hysterically probably. Bud the bartender just shook his head. Now I'm roaring, looking down at my beautiful, white veil like it is some kind of disfigured swan, just soothing its wounds and laughing, just crying and laughing and hugging my poor veil.

"What's going on, Kathy?" Shelly's hair was plastered against her face with sweat from being on the crowded dance floor. She was out of breath. "Oh, Kathy. Will you look at that? Balls. Fuckin' shame," she choked out breathlessly. "Is this the stupid bastard that ruined it?"

I was in stitches. I couldn't stop laughing. Tears ran down my cheeks. "No, Shelly, he's the stupid bastard," I croaked pointing to Jess who stopped laughing and just stood there looking scared as though demons from the pit of hell might burst through the ancient floorboards and swallow him at any second.

"I ain't never defiled no bride," he said pathetically, which made me laugh harder if that was possible. Bud, the bartender, grabbed my arm to stop me from falling off the barstool.

Bud looked at Shelly. "She always like this?" he asked her keeping a grip on my arm.

"Just jitters, I guess." Shelly sounded almost sober.

Jess dipped his head two or three times, "Be seein' ya ladies. Good luck with your weddin' and all." Then he hustled himself out the door. Bud let go of my arm to pour some water, which he held out to me. I swallowed but the giggles kept rising up. I took another swallow and finally they seemed to subside, at least until Shelly and I were outside in the fresh air. Then I started up again.

"You'd think you were the one drinkin'. You want me to drive?"

"God, no! Give me a minute." I looked down at my white satin shoes, now covered with brown dust. What was I thinking? What could I have been thinking? We got in the car but another fit of laughter rocked me. I wiped my nose with the back of my hand and sniffled.

"You about done?" Shelly lit a cigarette.

"Just give me a minute," I broke into laughter again. I held up my hand to let her know it was over—I was finished. I straightened my back, swallowed hard, and took a deep breath but fell into giggles again and banged my head against the steering wheel to try to get hold of myself.

"Look, Kathy, you get yourself together. I gotta pee. Open the window and let that cold air in. I'll be right back."

Watching her walk back into the bar was strangely sobering. For a split second I thought about driving away to I don't know where. Driving off. Throwing the veil and the shoes out the window, shoving my wedding dress out the back door of the car and just driving down the road to who knows where. It was cold and I started the engine, turned on the radio, cranked up the heater, and rolled up the window leaving it open only a crack. There was something about laughing so much that made me feel sick, made me feel spent. I wasn't really sure how far I could make it that night. I suddenly felt dog-tired; the muscles in my arms felt weak. The muscles in my legs quivered when I lifted them to take off my heels and throw them in the back seat. My regular shoes were in the trunk but I was too tired to get out of the car and get them.

I glanced at my watch. Shelly had been in there for at least ten minutes. She'd probably gotten back on the dance floor, beer in one hand, cigarette in the other, doing her slow hoochie-coochie dance. Or maybe some guy tempted her out the back door into his truck for a quick toke or a quick something else. Maybe she was in the john spewing out her guts. I didn't want to go in there. I'd have to put on some shoes and leave the warmth of the car, and I just didn't think I wanted to do that. I'd give her five more minutes.

Five minutes came and went and I was beginning to think something had happened. I didn't know what—some alien abduction, a bar fight. For God's sake, a town like Johnsonville, a bar in the middle of nowhere, men who have more muscles than brains. And a woman like Shelly. Now, there was a recipe for disaster.

I popped my trunk and turned off my engine. The pavement was frozen. One touch on the bottom of my foot sent me scampering to my open trunk. I perched myself on the side and pulled on my shoes, hopped out, slammed the trunk, and dashed for the bar.

Bud gave me an eyebrows-up jerk of his head when he saw me. I smiled back at him and then scanned the dance floor looking for Shelly. I moved through the crowd of tables resting my eyes on anyone with dirty blonde hair and a black t-shirt. Near the dance floor, it was almost easier to look for her boots than her face, but I didn't see either. The ladies room was off to the right just beyond the little bandstand. Six women were lined up waiting for the one-toilet room. She was in there; I knew it. From the looks of things, she'd probably been in there for fifteen or twenty minutes. I walked up to the door amid protests from the waiting women and I knocked hard on the door.

"Shelly! Shelly, you in there!" I yelled trying to get ahead of the music. No answer. "Ladies," I turned to the line, "I'm going to see if there's a key to open the door from this side. I'm sorry about this."

I made my way past the dance floor and caught Bud's attention.

"You seen my friend?" I asked him. "I think she may be in trouble in the john. You got a key?"

Bud fetched the key but didn't hand it over. "I'll have to unlock it myself," he told me raising the bar door and stepping out. I followed him to the ladies room door, which he opened. There was Shelly sound asleep on the john, her pants down around her ankles.

"Shelly!" I screamed at her inches from her face. Shelly didn't stir. I heard the line outside getting restless. "Com'on!" one yelled. "Smack that Bitch!" another urged. Another headed for the open door. "Drag her off that pot. I gotta go," she said marching in.

"Hold the door, Amy," Bud told the woman. "I'll gunny sack her." Bud strode over to Shelly, grabbed her beneath both arms and threw her over his shoulder. Her pants were still down around her ankles; I tried to pull them up but her legs were against Bud's chest, so I grabbed Bud's bar towel and covered her butt with it. To tell the truth, hardly anybody noticed Bud carrying Shelly past the dance floor, down the path through the tables, and out the door.

"This your car?" It was the only non-truck in sight. "Open the door and I'll throw'er in."

Shelly half-laid crumpled in the passenger seat. I rounded the car and climbed in the driver's side and started the engine. Bud fastened the seatbelt around Shelly, closing the car door and turning to head back to the bar.

I buzzed down the window, "Thanks, Bud."

"You're welcome." He hiked up his jeans, sniffed.

"Oh! You want your towel back," I yelled after him.

Bud turned, a little smile on his face. "No, you keep it." As he walked away, I heard him add, "You ladies come back real soon, hear?"

I should have thought to put a blanket in the

car. Shelly was in the passenger seat with nothing but a bar towel over her. Couldn't have been more than thirty degrees outside. I cranked up the heat, which immediately made me sleepy. There was a sign for a McDonald's six miles up the road. Maybe I could drive through for a cup of coffee without them seeing Shelly. On second thought, better that I crack my window and inhale the cold air.

Actually, she looked kind of pretty, my future kids' future Aunt Shelly. I didn't know how many miles were left but I liked the dark and the quiet and Shelly sleeping soundly beside me. I glanced back at my wedding dress that took up the entire back seat, the ruined shoes, the scorched veil. No doubt, life was going to be really interesting.

Aunt Tilly's Cure for Heartbreak

I admired Marion's grief. It was so genuine, so heartfelt. The way she straightened Steve's white collar and smoothed his tie as he lay in his coffin made us all turn away. I sat in the back, numbed by the thought that the ashes from Steve's cigarettes were still in an ashtray under the edge of my bed. The towel he'd used after his shower still hung on the towel rack.

It could be worse; I could be Marion's best friend and have to stand holding her hand, giving her water to make sure she didn't faint. I could be the one who had to beg her to take a break to eat just a bite. Stand next to his coffin with her. Lana is Marion's best friend; thank God for small favors. And, at least, Marion's husband didn't die in my bed. At least, he died in his own bed with his own wife next to him and that was a blessing. Things could have been worse.

I could bear watching Marion with her green eyes rimmed in red and hands that never stopped moving except when someone took them and held them to console her, quieting them for the moment. They all looked into her eyes as if they could see her soul. I could even bear watching her being gracious, being beautiful. She was lovely in her sadness; she was stunningly bereft. People are supposed to die and that's the truth. It isn't just their destiny; it's their duty. Maybe not at forty-four but people live and die. That's just what happens.

What I dreaded, what I was afraid I couldn't bear, was going back to Marion and Steve's house after the cremation tomorrow. In the funeral home, I could sit quietly and say little or nothing. But, tomorrow, I'd have to keep my hands from trembling while I sipped coffee. Tomorrow, I'd have to talk in a calm steady voice as though Steve and I were never close, were never lovers, but that I was only Marion's friend, somebody whose daughter played with her daughter, whose children had sleepovers together.

Lovers: that's the wrong term to describe Steve and me. We never loved each other. Steve's death was shocking because he was so young, so seemingly vigorous. At forty-four his hair was thick and black. He was strong; he worked out. The night he died, Marion's friend Lana told me that Steve had come in late from a meeting. He had chest pains and asked Marion to remind him in the morning to make an appointment. In another hour, though, he told Marion that she'd better call an ambulance. But Steve must have died when she left him to open the door for the paramedics. That's what she told Lana. The paramedics defibrillated him but he was irretrievably gone. Lana called to tell me the bad news and to let me know the funeral arrangements.

His "meeting" had been with me, of course. I don't know. There seemed to be something lucky about that. I mean getting to be with him one last time without even suspecting it was the last time, lucky because he went home to die. I shudder to think.

I wanted to leave the visitation in the middle somewhere. Not so soon as to have rushed out and not so late as to appear to linger. Two hours into it, with two hours left, I got up to say goodbye to Marion.

"You know if there's anything…" I told her, taking both her hands in mine and looking her in the eyes as others had done before me.

Marion let go of my hands and flung her arms around me sobbing into my neck. "Oh, Dannie, I miss him so much!" she said. "I don't know what I'll do without him." My first thought was, she knows; Marion knows. For a minute I panicked and wanted to disengage and run for the door. But, I stood there, letting Marion cry. I put my arms around her and rubbed her back as though that were some ancient remedy for grief. Marion sagged in my arms and Lana came to make sure Marion didn't crumple. Someone else brought a chair for her, and Lana sat her down and put a glass of water in her hand. Marion didn't look at me. Julie-Anne came to stand by her mother's side. That made it easy to slip out. After all, this wasn't about me. I had no grief really. I never loved Steve.

The funeral home, as all funeral homes, had been stifling and I was glad to get out into the night air. There was nowhere to go really. I didn't feel like sitting at home alone, so I ran through options in my head. The shopping mall was open for another hour. The movies were an option. I felt like having a drink but drinking alone in a bar…no, not for me. I was a little hungry. Everything felt awkward and just wrong. I wasn't mourning and I wasn't grieving but there was a kind of restlessness, a kind of heaviness in my chest. Without loss, how could I need comfort? But that's exactly what I needed — someone to comfort me.

As much as I'd be overwhelmed by the stillness, home was the best place for me. After the divorce, I had rented a small apartment in the city. I had not fought Curtis in his bid for primary custody of Ava. The woman who would become his second wife was already pregnant and Ava would have a loving home; I knew with certainty that Ava would be happier with her father. Besides, I was a wreck after the divorce. I quit my job impulsively and, even after a year's search, I hadn't been able to find a new one. Custody of Ava would have been selfish. So, it's mainly Aunt Tilly and me.

Aunt Tilly was a typical cat. Independent. Aloof. I'd gotten her from Tiger Lily, an organization for cats in danger of being euthanized. I was attracted to her because she pretended not to care about me, didn't look at me when I tried to catch her attention, indulged me when I wanted to pet her. She'd been in the shelter for a while, in a small cage. Somehow, we seemed suited to each other.

When I came through the door, Aunt Tilly barely raised her head. When I went to the kitchen and opened a can of food for her, she stretched, jumped off the sofa, and sauntered in to take her dinner.

I hadn't consciously made a decision to take a zip-lock bag out of the kitchen drawer and go into the bedroom to empty Steve's ashtray into it. That kind of act can't be planned. It's too absurd. The ashes spilled easily into the baggie; I zipped it closed. What an odd sight. His cigarette ashes were like a cremated piece of him, reduced, transformed.

Then, I went into the bathroom. Taking a large storage bag from the linen closet, I held Steve's towel up to my face to smell him one last time, folded it, and slipped it into the storage bag. Then I remembered something else. Steve's condom should still be in the trash bin. I had asked him not to flush them because the building was old and the plumbing was iffy. I picked the condom out of the trash with two fingers. This was like Steve, too, or like some shed skin of him. I took it to the kitchen, shook out another snack-size zip-lock bag and dropped in our condom. Here were the remains of Steve.

What to do with him now? Three baggies of Steve sat on my kitchen counter.

Pouring myself a glass of wine, I went to the living room and turned on the news. Aunt Tilly followed, climbing up on the couch when I sat down. I stroked her black fur. If I loved anything besides Ava, I loved Aunt Tilly.

"You have no idea how lucky you are, do you, my friend? No love affairs. No…well…no emotional needs at all." She purred as though she were proud of her superiority over her human. "People are so stupid, get ourselves into such… um …. situations."

On television, Ruth Madoff, wife of the infamous swindler Bernie, followed her husband through a confusion of news reporters, her face expressionless. I had turned off the sound and so what I saw was a woman caught up in her husband's misdeeds.

"See Aunt Tilly? Look. Look at her face. On the other hand," I turned up the sound a little, "her necklace is to die for. The point is, Aunt Tilly, you are not grieved by what you don't have. You want nothing and you have nothing. Even your litter box technically belongs to me. Your dish too.

Your husband will never break your heart by committing massive fraud or by dying and leaving you with two small kittens. You never have to worry about a roof over your head or food in your dish. You've found the perfect cure for heartbreak."

In the back of my mind, barely conscious thoughts of appropriate resting places for the baggies of Steve were being mulled. The real Steve wasn't yet disposed of, his body comfortably resting in its coffin in the airless funeral home until tomorrow. Still, my portion of Steve couldn't stay on my kitchen counter. There was the storage box under my bed. I could put him in with spare blankets and winter sweaters. Or, the top shelf of Ava's closet held only one box of toys she'd gotten too old for and her best baby clothes that could still be used. But those things smacked of the future, the next winter, a new husband someday. No, Steve needed buried with the past. There was a trunk in the storeroom downstairs containing among other things, a corsage from my first dance in high school, a yearbook, boxes of photos—yes, that's where Steve belonged. But…not yet. Not tonight. Maybe tomorrow. Tonight, he would be in his place beside me in our bed. Then, tomorrow…

Aunt Tilly got up, arched her back to stretch, and then moved to the far end of the couch to resettle. "Zen master Tilly," I said, turning up the sound again, "I'm learning. At least, I didn't love Steve."

The Book Finder

"Imagine the world without *The Diary of Anne Frank*," said Mr. Fowler. "Books, they're our hedge against forgetting. They're a way of understanding the world at a pace that actually allows comprehension, allows us to breathe and be at ease, be thoughtful. Not like the world we live in now, a world without books, at least not paper ones."

Mr. Fowler was a regular customer. He owned Pen and Ink, a fountain pen shop in the antique mall where I'd been renting an alcove since 2025, four years now. My shop was simple, three sides with no door to enter, just open to the rest of the mall. I had painted the walls a brick red and put a twentieth century cherry wood armoire to the side and a matching desk in the middle. The only thing on the desk was an arte nouveau cardholder with cards that read: Cynthia Carter, Book Finder.

It was hard to get used to a bookshop without books, but I'd been warned once already. It wasn't the books per se, but paper books that the vigilantes, a group fashioned after The Firemen in Ray Bradbury's book *Fahrenheit 451*, objected to. They wore a disc with a phoenix in the middle and a salamander on their sleeve like Bradbury's Firemen.

"I loved bookmarks! Didn't you?" Mr. Fowler's voice jarred me out of the place my thoughts had taken me. He was rhapsodic but I was ready to be annoyed by his use of the past tense, as though he no longer loved them. What he meant, of course, was that bookmarks were now something that had disappeared, that were, in fact, as obsolete as washboards. "I remember one bookmark," Mr. Fowler smiled a Cheshire Cat smile, "that was the shape of a cow and when you pressed a certain spot it mooed! The cow was black and white with a thin red ribbon holding a tiny gold bell around its neck." He held his fingers together to indicate its tininess. "I had a whole collection I kept in the plastic sleeves of a photo album and when I'd get a book, I'd pick out the bookmark that I thought was best suited, that had a kind of symbiosis with the book, as though they needed to love each other, be friends." He paused for a long while, eyes cast toward the ceiling, hands collapsed across his paunch. "*Heidi of the Alps*," he said wistfully. "The cow marked my place in *Heidi of the Alps.*" I thought he might be getting ready to leave; it was closing time for me, but then he went on, "I read *The Dairy of Anne Frank* when I was thirteen. Never forgot it. How can anyone forget a book like that?"

"Indeed, Mr. Fowler. Who can forget Anne Frank? But, you have a request? Is there something I can find for you?"

"Yes, yes!" Mr. Fowler fumbled in his jacket pocket with both hands and pulled out a perfectly oblong scrap of paper. He straightened the paper, smoothed it, and then looked closely at it. "I'm afraid I've given you quite a task this time."

"Let me see." I held out my hand for his scrap of paper but he seemed reluctant to turn it over. After a few more seconds of scrutiny, he handed me the paper.

It wasn't Mr. Fowler's handwriting, which was fluid and graceful and always written with one of his own precious fountain pens. This was almost illegible, scrawled across the paper in green ballpoint pen. Instinctively, I turned the paper over. There was nothing on the back but a smudge of something brownish. This was very unlike Mr. Fowler.

"I'm not sure what this says," I told him. "Is it something *Humming Bird*?"

"May I?" Mr. Fowler held out his hand and I returned the paper to him. "Hmmm, I think it says *A Cunning Bird*. See?" He pointed to the H that he saw as a C and the ms that he saw as ns.

"Who recommended the book to you? There's no author or date of publication."

"I told you this would be a devilish task." This made Mr. Fowler chuckle and then stifle the chuckle. "Actually, I ran across this scrap of paper in a book I was reading. It was tucked between the pages in the middle of the book as if to mark the reader's place. At first I just left it there but I became more curious as the days went by and decided to see if you might be able to locate this book for me."

"Are you sure it's a book? I mean this could refer to a person or a restaurant for all we know. It could be a reminder of something the reader needed to do."

"Well, Cynthia, I'm pretty certain that it's a

book; I feel it. Would you mind looking into it? Make a few phone calls? Rule out that it's a book? You don't seem very busy right now and I could pay you for your research."

Mr. Fowler did quite well with his pens. Besides, he'd been a good customer of my father and when my father died and I closed the bookshop, Mr. Fowler recommended that I rent a spot here.

I took the paper back from him and nodded. He was right; I wasn't busy, hadn't been busy for…well, never…I was never busy. My father's bookshop had been a popular meeting place off the main street in the heart of the city. It was big enough to have its own coffee shop where intellectuals and artists gathered. Now, books barely existed and I wondered if intellectuals and artists existed either. My father had opened the bookshop in the sixties when he was just twenty years old and he'd had a good run for more than half a century. Then, we entered the electronic age. Electronic books were fast over-coming print books and my father died just before the book publishers started to close their doors back in 2010. There are no books left to sell, no new ones anyway. Oh, there were still specialty publishers who produced a hundred copies of this or that, a memorial to a sainted mother, a celebration of a wedding to set on a coffee table, gift books not meant for the general reader. In the past several years, even used books, my livelihood, didn't make enough profit to pay my rent, so things weren't looking good for my current enterprise either. The mall owner gave me the space for a percentage just because the space, without walls, was pretty useless. I had a few regular clients, but finding books was expensive. Once, though, not a regular, Mr. Kaufman, sent me to Germany to bring back a number of books before the German titles were all in private collections. They were "esoteric" books he said and not likely to be transformed into digital copy. He'd feared they'd be lost forever like the ancient Egyptian scrolls in Alexandria, the cave-like library of stone shelves mysteriously ravaged by fire. And a few clients like Mr. Fowler came in from time to time asking for something long out of print or not available, at least not yet, in electronic form.

Besides, fewer and fewer people actually saw the value of reading. Books certainly had no advantage over the short, succinct entries one could find easily on-line, or so I'm told. Reading a book took too long and what was the point? I'm not quite old, I was born when my parents were in their forties, but I don't understand this. I don't understand how young girls reach adulthood without reading about Katherine and Heathcliff, about Anna and Vronsky. In two hundred years love stories are unchanged. They are never obsolete and they need the sensuality of the physical page. Without paper, Vronsky and Heathcliff are virtual lovers without the flesh of the page.

I got my coat and purse from the armoire and started walking through the mall to the exit. The Mall was open until nine in the evening but I closed at five, so as I walked, I passed open shops of china, fine jewelry, vintage clothes, and vinyl records in a shop that also sold stereos to play them on. Next to the music box shop was a teashop where weary shoppers could rest. Outside the shop was a cash machine that was already out of date because people were having credit chips implanted behind their ear. No one took cash anymore, in fact, paper money was no longer minted, but if a plastic credit card were produced, the shop owners grudgingly accepted it. A sale was a sale.

Usually, I stopped to look in the jewelry store window or to talk to Mrs. Bradshaw who owned the shop. We would commiserate over the fact that so many places were on-line market places and that only grocery stores managed to stay open, but the antique mall still existed because it was one of the few places that served as a gathering place, as markets all over the world always did from ancient times — biblical times — the agora. We had a small movie theater, albeit the movies were streamed, but people loved to come and sit in the large, dark theater as part of a popcorn-munching audience who laughed or cried in unison, reacting to the actors on the screen. An elegant chocolate shop was near the entrance so that people could stop in for a quick purchase. But, today, I was in a hurry and passed by barely peeking to see what Mrs. Bradshaw might be doing or what new piece might be displayed in her window. I was on my way to the Arkush library, which was selling off its stock. The library would stay open, but the book stacks would be replaced with electronic stations. The sale had started this morning and I'd probably already missed the best bargains. I flagged a taxi and told the cabbie my destination.

"The driverless cabs hit the streets today," the cabbie said when I had settled myself in the back seat. I'd heard something about it. I knew it was coming, but everything happened so fast or so it seemed.

"What are you going to do?" I asked him.

"Drive a cab. That's what I do." He looked at me in his rearview mirror.

"But, how can you compete with cab companies that don't have to pay a driver? Won't all the cabbies be put out of business?"

He shrugged his shoulders. "Nobody's going to save money on cabs," he almost smirked. "Didn't you hear? The rich just get richer. The price will be the same whether there's a driver or not. Who passes manufacturing savings on to the customer? Nobody. But more people will be out of work, and the people at the top will just make more profit."

Somehow I felt that the driverless cabs were going to meet with some odd collisions like cartoons in which pianos fell mysteriously from the sky.

"Some of my friends have already moved to a commune. Self-sustained: built their own houses, grow their own food, make what they need."

I could only see his eyes in the rearview mirror and he was hard to read. I couldn't tell if it was pride or fear in his voice.

"Sounds a little scary!" I said.

His eyes were back on the road but I could see

that his forehead had turned into a mass of furrows he could almost plow. He shrugged. We went the rest of the way in silence. We passed an invaded house. Scrawled in big letters on the exterior wall was the word "LUDDITE." The street was still scorched where the books had been set afire. The Firemen had been there. I'd heard, but I hadn't seen before. When we stopped, he tried to scan my ear before I could hand him my plastic card.

It was silly, but I missed the feel of money, it's dirtiness from being passed from one hand to another, slapped into dirty register drawers, wadded in pockets and shoved into wallets. Money had history. I missed the stacks of bills my father brought home from book buyers who paid cash. I missed coins. Jars of pennies. A dollar under a pillow from the tooth fairy. I missed dropping quarters into a slot and then pressing a button to see my candy bar drop into the tray. I missed twenty-dollar bills tucked inside the birthday card from my grandmother. Something tactile was disappearing. I missed books that you felt the heft of and that left your fingers dry turning pages, cab drivers who told you their gripes from the time you got in until the time you got out, the almost sensual character of money where you could tell the difference between a lot of money and a little money by the space it took — that was all gone and the world was diminished.

There was no line trailing from the library book sale to the stairs outside. The building looked abandoned except that the lights were on but barely a soul could be seen. Inside, in the main library room where the librarians had been replaced by computer technicians who helped library users retrieve books from clouds and download them to other devices, there were only a few people perusing the book tables. The stacks had already been taken away, but boxes of books were stored under the tables ready to be brought up when a bare spot appeared.

"Cynthia!" Lysella was young and full of energy. She dressed in the androgynous fashion of the day, shaved head, a modern version of the Mao jacket, and storm trooper boots. "I thought you'd be here earlier. I set some things aside for you that I thought might be of interest. Come and look."

I touched Lysella's cheeks with my cheek, smiled, and followed her to her office where she'd accumulated about fifteen books that sat in two stacks on the corner of her desk. I picked up the first one.

"Anything you can use?" she asked.

Suddenly, I was overwhelmed and felt weak. I backed-up a few steps and collapsed into the nearest chair.

"Cynthia, what is it! Are you un-well?"

I shook my head finding it difficult to speak.

"I'll get some water," she said hustling out of the room.

When she returned, I had recovered a little. "Lysella," I asked her, "did you ever read *Fahrenheit 451*?"

"Of course! Doesn't everybody? Why?" It took Lysella only a second to connect things. "Sweetie, books aren't gone. Nobody hates books. They're only transformed. I mean, it's better, isn't it? They can never be destroyed now. No one can burn them. You can't accidentally leave them anywhere. They're safe, Cynthia, perfectly safe." She had been leaning against her desk but now she sat down next to me.

"You know what I like so much about books?" I asked not expecting an answer, "I like turning the pages and getting to the middle of the book so that you can see, even feel in your hands, that you are exactly in the middle. And then, one side gets lighter and one side gets heavier, a shifting of weight as I move through the book." I felt bereft really, as though something I loved was dying. "If you were a book, Lysella, what book would you be?"

She laughed, "I'll give you an answer next week!"

I wondered if I'd be back next week when all the tables would be gone and not one paper book remained in the library.

I took a sip of water. "I came over in a cab and the driver was talking about communes and I couldn't help but think of *451*, the people wandering the woods repeating the books they'd memorized."

"The world is changing," Lysella said, "and it ought to change. People have felt like you for as long as there was civilization. I'm sure when paper was invented, someone was bemoaning it's fragility and claiming the superiority of indestructible stone tablets! Someone no doubt missed the horse manure in the streets when everyone began to drive cars. Don't be a luddite, Cynthia! I know big, clunky books are your thing, Sweetie, but you've got to move with the times."

She was right, I knew she was right, but she was also wrong. I smiled weakly, gathered myself together, and spent the next hour going through the library tables, placing the books I wanted in a box to be delivered to my house the next day. My heart just wasn't in it, though. What was I doing hopelessly clinging to a life that was fast disappearing? Why was I lugging home books to a house already stuffed to the gills with them? If library patrons didn't want to read real books even for free, what made me think I could sell them?

I'd asked Lysella to do some research on *My Hummingbird* or *A Cunning Bird* and before I left, I checked back with her.

"Well, there's several books called *The Hummingbird*, most of them about how to attract and feed them in your yard, but nothing on *My Hummingbird*. I did find one novel; the listing shows the title as *Hummingbird,* no 'the' or 'my.' Nothing under cunning bird. Could it be *The Running Bird*? I found a listing for that title."

I asked her to send the two novels to my computer and went home. I was strangely spent. What had been tiring about the day I couldn't pinpoint. I was exhausted — emotionally exhausted. Inside my apartment building, the electricity, now controlled by the National Centralized Energy Corporation, had failed again. No elevator. I walked up three flights. I held the handrail; the stairwell was dark. The security cameras had a back-up system, though, and I felt safe; the only people around were people like me coming home from work or kids using it as an opportunity to have sex under the dark stairwells. Without electricity, the optical scanner on my front door didn't work, so I resorted to my key and the small flashlight attached to my key ring.

Every available space in my apartment was already used for book storage. Last year, I'd gotten rid of my bed frame and placed my mattress on a platform of books. Tables were piles of books with glass or board tops; columns of books held lamps. The storage closet in the basement, the guest bathroom, the top of the fridge, everywhere was covered with books. And more were coming tomorrow.

What was I doing? I was on the fast track to insanity. Trying to hold onto the world as I knew it, trying to reverse the clock, go back to non-G.M.O. foods, and furniture constructed only with natural materials--what good was all this effort? I couldn't change one thing.

The electricity flickered and my refrigerator began to hum. I turned on some lights. Sitting down with a sandwich, I opened the one book I'd brought home with me from the library, *The Infinities*, by John Banville. I opened the book and read his first line: "Of the things we fashioned for them that they might be comforted, dawn is the one that works." How perfectly exquisite! First person narrative from a god's point of view! Brilliant! I'd read the book twenty or more years ago, and again when I found a copy in a bookshop in England ten years ago. I'd forgotten the delicacy of the opening line, its lyricism. When I ask myself what I'm doing, I know that what I'm doing is for the sake of John Banville's first line. The book is almost human with its pliable pages that can be torn, burned, kissed, written on, that can be held, that can die and rot like a human. The book is the mind of John Banville and it seems so. In those pages, John Banville has poured out his mind like thick, rich cream. The words did not come from an inorganic machine, but from a human brain. And, I do it for every poet who ever lived, even the bad ones, but especially for the good ones like Billy Collins who wrote about *Aimless Love* saying that he fell in love with a wren, and a bowl of broth, and a bar of soap because he was full of love for the world.

I do it for today's writers who will never have a book on the shelf in the library or in a bookstore, will never have a book for which I will search, but only have air books in cyber-space, books in clouds someplace.

I slept fitfully throughout the night and the next morning, I waited for the books to be delivered from the library. I stacked books higher or pushed them tighter to make room for yet another pile, and I thought about renting a storage unit. This thought was constant, but where would I get the money? When I had made what I thought would be sufficient space, I looked at the books Lysella had sent, *The Running Bird* and The *Hummingbird,* but I could see right away that these were not books that would interest Mr. Fowler. *The Running Bird* was a Dr. Suess-ish tale of a roadrunner and *The Hummingbird* told the story of the building and first flight of a small plane.

The books came, I catalogued them, and arrived at my alcove a little past noon. A young woman was waiting when I arrived with a book in hand she hoped to sell to me. The book, though, was not rare and no one would hire a book finder to locate a book like this. It was written in 2020 by an African writer. African writers had been much in vogue in the last decade or so. The oddity of the book was not that it was an African author, but that the book was not electronic but paper, produced by an African publishing house on paper made from processed elephant dung. Africa was producing paper books because it had lots of natural materials to manufacture paper. In the last twenty years, most Africans had become literate, but many people were still in non-computerized households. Still, I told her no, the book was available online and most people preferred it online. I didn't feel I could sell a hard copy. She looked a little downcast and I assured her that the book had some value, just not to me.

The only other customer was a man who came in looking for a First Edition copy of a Mark Twain book. These were rare because they'd all been bought up long ago for private collections or private reading rooms. That, and the vigilante book-burners targeted anything that had been deemed classic. I didn't have the book, I told him, and didn't think I could get it, but, if he'd give me his name and address, I'd message him if I got my hands on one.

I filled that day and the next making calls to all my contacts, booksellers around the world but I couldn't find a shred of evidence that such a thing as *A Hummingbird, My Hummingbird*, or *The Hummingbird* existed. There was a massive university library in the United Scandinavian Territories but nothing turned up that I could use. If they didn't have it, it didn't exist I was sure. An esoteric note in an old and unpopular book—I was probably wasting my time.

Then, I got a note from Lysella saying she had spoken to a woman named Jennifer Mooney and that I would be hearing from her. She didn't elaborate; the library had become busier than ever. It took a couple more days before I got mail from Jennifer Mooney saying she'd like to meet. "It's taken me some time to make this decision," she wrote. "but I need to do this to honor my husband. Can you meet me at the teashop near your alcove tomorrow at 5?"

I was oddly excited as I walked to the teashop the next day. I didn't know whom I was meeting but Jennifer Mooney said that she'd seen me at work and would have no problem recognizing me. When I walked into the teashop, a tiny, frail woman raised a gloved hand and waved.

Approaching her was like walking into a hot house full of orchids. There was something beautiful and rare about her, something so melancholy that it pervaded the air long before I'd reached the table. She wasn't an old woman, maybe seventy I'd guess, but she had the air of someone ancient, as though she had lived many centuries and I was totally enchanted by her before she spoke a word.

"I'm Cynthia Carter," I said feeling foolish already. She knew who I was.

"Yes," she said. "I'm Jennifer Mooney. Please call me Jen."

I sat down. There was an empty cup in front of me and a silver teapot big enough for both of us. Jen was drinking from a thin china cup so delicate I could see through it. I asked her how she knew Lysella.

"I was a school teacher," Jen told me, "and I relied on Lysella so much! I used to take every class on a field trip to the library as part of the life-long learning curriculum. I wonder if teachers still do that."

As I watched her, she seemed to light up. The pale skin of her face seemed to take on color and vibrancy.

She was in no hurry. I settled back and refilled my cup.

"I knew your father; my husband and I frequented his shop. My husband was quite the booklover." It was as if someone had flipped a switch in her. Her eyes took on a sparkle, the pale blue seemed now like sapphire.

"You knew my father?"

"Yes, and you were probably that little girl who was always messing about! I was a bride of twenty and you seemed to me about eight or so then." I quickly did the math. She looked much older than late fifties. "We lived not far from the bookshop in those days" she continued, "and often went in on Sunday morning for breakfast and to read the newspaper your father offered for free." She laughed then, a girlish giggle that startled me and made me smile. "Oh, but you are surely busy and I'm keeping you. We ought to get down to business. But first I must ask you who requested *My Hummingbird*? Who knows such a book exists?

"First, let me assure you that I'm in no hurry. I would just be back in my dull apartment eating my nightly cheese sandwich so I'm delighted to stay as long as you can spare. To answer your question, a man named Mr. Fowler came to me with the request."

"Fowler? I don't know this man." She lifted her gloved hand and took a little sip. Her gloves were lace and immaculately white. She was sort of retro-fashionable. Although everyone had taken to wearing gloves these days to prevent the spread of disease, seldom were they white lace.

"He has a fountain pen shop here in the mall," I told her. "He had run across a slip of paper in a book that he was reading. The slip of paper had the words *My Hummingbird* written on it in green ball point pen."

"Oh!" She covered her surprised mouth. "Where did he get that book?"

"I'm not sure, but I would guess he bought it from me. It was in my father's shop and ended up being stored in my apartment. I'm always glad…no, grateful…when someone relieves me of a book stored in my apartment!"

"Oh, I see now," she said. "I must have sold that book to your father, let's see, almost three decades ago. I thought I'd taken all those slips of paper out of the books, but I guess I missed one."

I cocked my head to one side. There was more that she wanted to say.

"My husband used to call me his hummingbird," she explained. "He said that I was like a little hummingbird, so small with hands that fluttered like hummingbird wings. We both read obsessively. He wanted to be a writer, a poet. He would put bookmarks labeled My Hummingbird to mark passages he thought I would like."

I sat back then. The hummingbird was sitting in front of me. "There's no book then? You're the hummingbird?"

"Oh, certainly there's a book and I'll show it to you in a bit. There's a book all right. I wish there didn't have to be such a book."

I couldn't speak then. I felt the depth of the melancholy that engulfed her, that swirled around her, that she sat, unmovable, in the midst of. I waited for her to continue.

"Jason Mooney, my husband, was a waiter in a restaurant called Windows on the World in the North Tower of the World Trade Center. In 2001, when the planes attacked the building, the North Tower was hit at 8:44 in the morning. The planes flew into floors 93, 94, 95, 96, 97, 98, and 99." She said each number distinctly as though she were calling out the names of the dead. "Windows on the World was on the top floor, 107, and so was cut off from any means of escape. No one knows what happened, of course, but I can imagine that Jason sat there, maybe from 8:44 when the tower was first hit until 10:28 when the tower collapsed, knowing that it was impossible for anyone to save the people who were on that floor. Everyone was doomed. Jason, a writer to the end, wrote poetry those last two hours and fourteen minutes of his life, poetry to me."

The building had been hit, was collapsing with thousands of people inside. The iron structure of the building was melting from the heat of the explosion, the fuel tanks from the airplanes that crashed into the ninetieth floors. How could a mere piece of paper have survived?

Jen read my mind.

"Jason had a metal container, a cookie tin, and…I can't figure it out…he must have thrown it off the building, maybe from the deck somehow or from a broken window. It wasn't found for weeks, maybe months, after 9/11, but one day a fireman came to my door with the cookie tin in his hand, a miracle he said. Jason had written a note to the finder asking him to please deliver the box to our address. Jason apologized for not having time to edit the poem, to illuminate the page as he often did when he wrote something especially for me. Somehow, the poem survived." Then, she rummaged in her handbag on the chair next to her and pulled out a small volume. "Maybe this is the most precious book in the world. I had five made, but I think there's only one now. This one."

Hers was an amazing story; I was speechless.

"This Mr. Fowler," she poured more tea, "what's he like?"

I blinked. What was Mr. Fowler like? I'd never thought about it really.

"Is he a collector?" she asked.

"Yes: he's been a good customer for a long time. Not just a collector, but a book lover. I mean someone who truly values books. I guess he's a nice man, an honest man…"

"Is he a generous man?" she interrupted, "Is he a loving man?"

I thought a minute. "No, I don't think he's either one of those things. He's curious, loves a mystery, a puzzle. He's thoughtful in his own way." I couldn't tell if that satisfied her.

"Is he lonely? Is he married?"

"I don't know, really. He's a long time customer but not a friend." That seemed to say a lot. Here's a man I've seen most days for at least four years but I didn't know much about him and I didn't consider him a friend.

Then she offered the book to me, holding it in both hands, and inching it toward me almost reluctantly.

It was a simple act that moved me — extending those gloved hands waiting for me to receive her precious gift. Maybe it was the magical aura of the shiny black book in her lace-covered hand, the too feminine, too fragile, white hand and the masculine, glossy black of the slim volume. What was handed to me seemed more than the mere transference of an object; it seemed more the passing from one human to another of a tremendous sorrow. Suddenly, I was afraid as though I was being offered to take into my possession something so burdened by grief that I would be crushed by it.

"You take it," she almost whispered. "You decide if Mr. Fowler is the right person. You'll know what to do."

I set the book down on the table in front of me and took a sip of tea. I was stalling. I looked at the book and near the top right corner a blue hummingbird was embossed. Jen seemed not even to breathe and kept her eyes glued to the book while I looked into her face. It was a strange kind of panic. My mind buzzed: did she intend to sell the book? Was Mr. Fowler merely curious or did he intend to buy this book? If she would sell and he would buy, did I really need even to open the book myself? How could a book of poetry be so daunting?

"Do you intend to sell this book, Jen?" I asked her.

"No, not sell," she said finally looking up from where her eyes had rested on the book. "but give it if you think it will help…"

"Help? Help who?"

"Survivors?" her voice was weak and questioning. Then, in a stronger voice, "People who have lost a loved one. People who have lost faith in love. In humanity. I don't know. People."

Even if this was the book Mr. Fowler was looking for, this was not a book that Mr. Fowler should own. That was easy to tell. I hadn't opened it yet, hadn't read the poems, but I knew that satisfying the curiosity of a stranger was not a good enough reason for Jen Mooney to part with the book. I was horrified to think of it even among the stacks in my apartment, e pluribus unum. This was a loved book, a treasure, an icon of history. It belonged in the museum where the twin towers used to stand. It needed to be honored.

"I take it you have the original poems?"

"Of course. In Jason's own hand. I keep them in the battered cookie tin that Jason put them in. When I die, those will go to the 9/11 museum."

I was relieved.

"Wouldn't you like to read them?" she asked me, touching the book again and nudging it toward me.

Actually, I wouldn't. I mean, not now, not in this place; the place was too public and the poems too private. I managed a smile. "Can I take them with me for a few days?"

I could tell by her face that taking the book away would be painful and yet there was also pain in my not taking it. When she didn't respond,

I said, "I shouldn't have asked. It's too precious."

"Still," Jen said, "if it would help. It is neither Jason nor his hand. It is only a book of poems that I put together myself. I can certainly do it again if need be."

After another cup of tea, we parted promising to meet in a week, same time, same place. I tucked the book in a pocket in the folds of my skirt.

It didn't seem right, me with that book, carrying it to my house with the masses of other books, a crowd like the Pope sees in Rio. Still, I was tired and hungry and surely the book wouldn't mind spending a week among its own kind.

The electricity was once again not working and I climbed the stairs in the dark. Inside, my apartment was stuffy as it often was with so much paper around. The electricity must have been off for a while; the cheese was warm and limp inside the fridge and the ice had melted in its bin. An apple that had been in the fridge for a month and some peanut butter would be my dinner. I decided to watch old footage of the destruction of the twin towers. I tapped in 9/11/2001 and within seconds my wall screen was awash with light. Since it was satellite, the fact that the electricity was out made no difference, and the screen ran on its own battery power. Because the wars in the Middle East were still being waged, there was easy access to this footage. I remembered, though. I was twelve when the airplanes struck the tower and I was getting ready for school. As usual, my mother had the television on and my father was fussing at her for disturbing his morning peace. This was a constant battle between them; this morning, though, the programming was interrupted so we could see with our own eyes this otherwise unbelievable news. The entire nation froze not knowing where the next attack would be. The three of us stayed glued to the set for hours. Now, I watched once again as the south tower was hit, as one tower crumbled and then the other.

I imagined Jason Mooney huddled in a corner writing his last words to his Hummingbird. I turned off the screen, picked up the book, and opened to the first poem. Jason begins:

> I loved the world through you,
> Loved the world you made for me
> With your hummingbird hands.

I imagined the smoke filling his lungs, the heat rising from the floors below, but I couldn't imagine what it might be like waiting to die. I didn't want to imagine it. I wondered how I would choose to spend time knowing they are the last minutes on Earth. Jason Mooney spent his last minutes honoring the life he shared with his wife and lamented that he would have to leave her behind in this world while he moved to the next, both of them lost without the other. He writes:

> This I know: love
> Speaks my name in your
> Whisper.

Jen Mooney collected his poems, brought them together and named the volume after Jason's pet name for her, his beloved. Love never goes out of fashion.

I was so enrapt in the pages of the book that it took me a good half-minute of utter confusion when my door burst open and two men and a woman rushed in. I bolted up, my heart racing and I shoved Jen's precious book into my skirt pocket. They didn't speak but began snatching up books and throwing them out my windows.

I was aghast, but I wasn't surprised. I'd been waiting for them, in a way. They were inevitable. I knew they wouldn't hurt me; they just wanted to reform me, bring me into the twenty-first century. Still, I could have or should have hidden the books in some off-the-beaten-track storage unit. There was no use now trying to stop them. Nothing I said or did would change anything. I collapsed down into the couch again and tried to pick up my phone without catching their eye. I could try to mitigate my damage by calling the police. One of them wrenched my phone out of my hand, though, and threw that out the window too. On his chest, woven into the fabric, was the now familiar disc with a phoenix in the center, on his sleeve, a salamander.

    They moved with practiced, drill-like efficiency, not speaking, handling my books like so much rank trash. Out my window, in the middle of my street, the smoke from the bonfire began to rise up, to waft into the room where I sat barely breathing. One of the intruders pulled away my mattress and began taking armfuls of books to the window. I tried to think; where had I stored the first editions? Where were the philosophy books, the poetry? Where was Joan Didion? Stanley Elkin? But the books weren't organized, just shoved in where I could open a space. Someone must have called the police. I heard sirens getting closer.

"Torch it and let's get out of here!" one of them commanded.

In unison, three hands pulled out three mini-firebombs, and then the three scurried out of the apartment and down the stairs. In seconds the firebombs would go off. I was paralyzed momentarily thinking how I could save the books but then I realized I would be lucky to save myself. Before I was out the door the first firebomb ignited the remainder of the books that had been my bed. I was halfway down the stairs when the second and third bombs went off.

The tenants had rushed out of my building and were standing among the crowd that had gathered. The bonfire in the street was just ash and smoldering remnants of hard covers and singed and charred pages. The police began shoving us over to the sidewalk across the street to make way for the fire truck. They were asking the crowd if they knew if anyone was still in the building.

Making my way to a police officer, I told him that it was my apartment that was on fire.

Hours past and slowly the people who had someplace to go went there. The blaze was contained but one fire truck remained to monitor the ashes, to make sure the smoldering paper would not re-ignite. A police car remained and another took me down to the station to make a statement. It was two in the morning before a policeman asked me where he could drop me, but I had to tell him there was no place. My purse had burned up with the books and I didn't have an implanted chip so I had no money at all and no phone. He told me that he could take me to a shelter for the night and I could figure things out in the morning, but when we walked outside the station, there was a man leaning against his cab. He stirred when he saw me and came over to us.

"Remember me?" he asked almost cheerfully.

I nodded. I remembered him…the cabbie…but what was he doing here? Was he waiting for me? Why?

"Come on," he said. "I'll take you home."

"My home is gone," I told him.

"Yes, I know," he took my arm, "that home is gone. I'll take you home."

"What?" I couldn't understand what he meant.

"We've kept an eye on you, Ms. Carter," he said still holding my arm. "We knew you were vulnerable. It was just a matter of time."

"Who? Who's been keeping an eye on me?"

"Friends," he said as though that explained

anything.

"You know my name, friend; what's yours?"

"Jimmy. I'm Jimmy." He was holding my arm, but we weren't moving. "We've been expecting you, Ms. Carter. Please come."

At this point I had little alternative. Besides, there was something about Jimmy, something I trusted. I nodded to the police officer who told me to keep in touch. He'd let me know when it was safe to go into my apartment again to see what I could salvage.

The cabbie…Jimmy… opened the door letting me slide into the back seat. I was exhausted.

"It's a little ways," he said. "Why don't you lean back and rest?"

"Are we going to that place? You talked about a place…" I was already half asleep.

"Yes. I told them about you and they're waiting. There's a cottage for you. I think you'll like it."

I had *My Hummingbird* in my skirt pocket. I was too tired to think about what books I might salvage or the basement storage area. I was too tired to think about the three vigilantes. I had in my mind, though, a little cottage in the woods in a village of people who valued books and storytelling and making things with their hands. I dreamed that there would be a garden of vegetables and flowers that I could see from a window.

The Last Race

Libby finished tossing Frankie's clothes out the window of their third floor apartment onto the common lawn and even, carried by the summer breeze, into the peaceful blue expanse of the swimming pool. Then, she turned her attention to his record collection. This ejection of Frankie's worldly goods was a kind of vomiting, retching up the sickness of what she once laughingly referred to as their relationship. She had tried lobbing his favorite Nikes into the pool, but falling short, the first shoe hit the fence and slid down along the metal weave to the ground where it lay like a dead cat. The second shoe was launched with much more ferocity but hit the fence as well, bouncing away, down a little slope, and onto the sidewalk.

She knew that she would find even greater satisfaction with his vintage vinyl. Frankie was a meticulous collector, laying the records flat rather than standing them like books on a shelf, and placing the stacks in a cool, dry, and dark closet, organized by genre, then alphabetically by artist, and then by recording date. It was a thing of beauty! Nothing could have given Libby more pleasure than the total destruction of his coveted collection. Not tidy by nature, Frankie's socks and underwear littered the bathroom floor where he shed his work clothes leaving them for Libby to pick up, but he pampered and prized each glossy black platter tending it as though its worth were staggering. It wasn't, especially to Libby.

*

Frankie walked away from the track where the dust settled from the second race. Trojan Victory, a young but proven gelding, had a winning jockey as its rider. Still, the horse's post-position wasn't the best and he'd raced just the night before. Given the competition, though, Frankie had no doubts that Trojan Victory would blow away every last nag, a rabbit in a snail's race. Frankie had been wrong, but not unlucky. He walked towards the ticket windows and away from the oval where the horses still trailed out back to their stalls. He looked down at his losing ticket, making sure that it was, in fact, a losing ticket, then ripping it first in two then again, and letting the pieces drift to the concrete like dying moths. It's only the second race, he thought to himself. There are six more tonight. This cheered him. He wouldn't lose three in a row — no way! No matter which one he chose, that horse was going to be the winner. He felt that in his bones.

Stepping up to Window 6, he was confronted with a new face, a long-haired, tattooed, young man in a red and black plaid, short-sleeved shirt and a shimmery green tie.

"Where's Chester?" Frankie felt a little panic rising. This could be bad luck. This new guy was young, inexperienced. He always bought tickets from Chester. Still, this was Window 6. The blasting of the air conditioners and the humming of the cash drawers seemed to calm him. "Something wrong with Chester?"

The new guy had a name badge with Guy written on it. He shrugged. "Got a call. Left." He didn't look up but kept his eyes on the cash drawer, making sure that all the denominations were in their correct slots.

"American Gold Star to win," Frankie told Guy, sliding a small stack of ones under the bars.

Guy was all business; he slid Frankie's ticket back toward him.

"Whadaya think of American Gold Star?" It was a plea really. What Frankie wanted to hear him say was that it was a wise choice and the horse was sure to win. That's not what he said, of course.

Guy shrugged. "Makes no difference what I think, buddy. You just bought the ticket. This transaction's over."

Frankie laughed a little and backed away almost bumping into the man behind him. The man behind Window 6 was right, of course. It didn't matter what the ticket seller thought. Frankie knew he was lucky and that's all he needed to know. Nobody loses three times in a row, especially not Francis Burke O'Neal. This time, I've got a winner, he told himself. It's almost a sure thing.

He bought a beer and went back to his seat.

*

Libby got a bottle of beer from the fridge. She had a Ray Charles in her hand and was reading the list of songs on the back cover. She liked this record, liked it a lot, but she was gleefully going to fling it out the window, maybe see how far it would sail. She leaned for a minute out the open window, catching the slight breeze that blew clouds across the night sky, hiding then revealing an absolutely white half moon. Two boys (she couldn't see them well enough to see whether they were men or boys) were holding some of Frankie's shirts, looking up at the window, then down at the shirts again, murmuring to each other.

"Hey! Hey!" Libby yelled at them. The two boys picked up a few more things and broke into a slow run. "No! Don't run away! Come back! You're welcome to that stuff. In fact, hey, you want an X-Box?"

The boys stopped like they'd hit a wall and looked up at Libby who smiled at them, Juliette looking down from her balcony.

"How old?" one of the boys yelled back.

Little fuckers. "What the hell difference does it make? It's free! Come on up here and I'll give it to you. I'm not joking. I'll give you an X-Box. You don't want it, sell it. I don't care."

The two boys put their heads together, looking up at her, talking to each other in low voices, then looking up again, "What apartment you in?"

*

American Gold Star came in a dismal fifth. Third race down, five to go. It was almost like a rerun, Frankie looking down at his ticket, ripping it twice, letting the pieces float to the floor that was increasingly obscured by losing tickets. There was something lucky about Window 6 where the guy with the plaid shirt and shimmery green tie took the money and returned the ticket. Guy was the one to buy from for the fourth race even though there was a longer line than at any other window. Word's out that Window 6 is the lucky window, Frankie reasoned. He waited for the line to diminish while he studied the racing form. He was torn between two entries, King Henry the Eighth and Purity's Beast. King Henry had a good jockey but one who hadn't won a race this week. He was due. On the other hand, Purity's Beast had a good jockey too but one who was just coming off an injury. Purity's Beast had a better position at the gate and she hadn't raced all week, which meant she was rested. That horse had won only once in her last six races, but placed twice. King Henry, though, had raced twice this week being ridden by a different jockey, placing in one race and showing in the other. It was a toss up really. He thought King Henry had better statistics by a slight edge but he had a gut feeling about Purity's Beast.

This time, Frankie asked about the horse before he bought the ticket. "Whataya you know about Purity's Beast?"

"Nothin'. If I knew somethin', I'd buy tickets not sell'em." Guy told him. "Look, buddy, it's a horse race. You win some; you lose some. You want to bet on Purity's Beast or not?"

"Yeah." Cold bastard! Frankie slid his wager toward the guy; the guy slid a ticket toward Frankie.

Only a loser loses four in a row, Frankie thought. And I'm no loser. I got an unerring gut and my gut's telling me that Purity's Beast is a winner.

By the time Frankie got back to his seat, the horses were all in their gates. Purity's Beast seemed restless, literally champing at the bit. The bell sounded, the gates opened, and the horses poured out, each jockey looking for the path to advance.

Jo Rousseau

*

Libby opened the door to the two boys who, in the light of the stairwell, looked older than she first thought. They seemed to be too old for the baggy shorts, over-sized t-shirts, and shower shoes they wore. One of them had hair that was already receding while the other's hair covered his eyes. She decided not to let them in.

"Wait here. I'll get it for you," she told them closing the door. She'd already unhooked the cables but the box was heavier than she expected. Nonetheless, she struggled to get it to the door. Back at the door, the two guys had come in; she had neglected to lock the door but it looked like it was locked now. One was standing in front of the door and Libby could hear the other in her kitchen. She could hear him rifling through the silverware drawer and she knew immediately what he was looking for.

"What's going on?" Libby flooded, terrified into paralysis. Her heart flashed like a disco ball. She was barefoot, in cut-offs and a tank top with no underwear on at all. It had been hot in the apartment because she'd turned off the air and opened the window. She'd drawn up her hair in a ponytail. "Take what you want and get out of here," she managed to choke out.

"Oh, we intend to take what we want all right." He was confident, cocky. He stared her down until she staggered back a step.

The other man returned from the kitchen and Libby's instincts had been right on target. He had two knives and gave one to the man who stood between Libby and the door. Usually her cell was in her back pocket, but she had no idea where it was now. She had no landline and her best option was to try to stir up some neighbors with her screams. Still, each man had a knife and she wouldn't last long if she tried that. Maybe she could talk her way out of this.

"My boyfriend will be back any minute," she told them unconvincingly. "He just went out for cigarettes." She felt like every nerve in her body was on high alert, wildly sending signals to run, to scream, to fight.

"Looks to me like you two had a helluva lover's quarrel. I'm guessin' even if he comes back, he's not coming up unless he's coming to mess you up. In that case, we're doin' 'im a favor."

Now, Libby's survival instincts awakened. She sounded more confident than she felt. "We were fighting over him infecting me with AIDS. That bastard! The prick gave me AIDS. You know what that is, don't you? AIDS! You know how that changes your life? One drop of my blood on you could kill you. You should get out of here before it's too late."

*

The fourth race and the fifth race were worse than the first three. Purity's Beast came in a brutal second, leaving Frankie to hope until the last second. He thought it was worse than not even being close—the disappointment was infinitely sharper, the cut so much deeper. At least that's what he thought until the fifth race when Oliver's Dream couldn't be coaxed from the gate, but reared and balked until the other horses rounded the first bend. Then the jockey, out to punish the horse, drove him mercilessly around the track as hard as the horse could go but gaining not one length on the horses far ahead of him.

Frankie didn't tear his ticket this time, but let it fall to the ground while he was still in his chair, his knees a little spread, his hands hanging loosely between them, and letting the ticket fall as though accidently. That was the fifth race: three more to go. But Frankie didn't think of it as time running out. He felt that his luck was as strong as ever, simply squeezed into the last three races, compressed instead of parsed out over all eight. Up to this time, he'd bought tickets only to win but now he wanted to change strategy; he couldn't manage all the fancy footwork of an exacta or trifecta, so he would buy a ticket to show giving the horse room to come in first, second, or third. This time, he would leave the choice to blind luck. Closing his eyes and circling the pencil three inches above the page, Frankie stabbed the racing form. He opened one eye and then the other: Son of Zeus, a horse that had never won a race but did show a time or two. He didn't consider himself a superstitious man, but he did consider himself a man singled out for special treatment by fate, although he wouldn't in a million years have said so out loud. Frankie also changed ticket windows, selecting the window with the shortest line. Behind the bars was somebody's grandma; a woman, who looked to Frankie, like something beyond seventy. At first, he thought that was a bad sign and almost decided to thank her and move to a different window. He was pretty sure, though, that whoever or whatever guided him knew best, had his best interests at heart, and if the powers that be wanted him to buy a ticket from granny then he'd buy a ticket from granny.

"Son of Zeus to show," he told her.

"Good luck," she said, "I hope it's a winner for you."

That sealed it. Race six was his race.

*

The two men were amateur punks. They called each other by name: Mack and Ben. They seemed not to care about fingerprints, although they touched nothing except the knives. They were in no hurry in her thin-walled apartment, didn't seem concerned about noise or what could be seen through the window, which was probably very little from the ground. She guessed they already knew that. Their carelessness signaled to her that they had no intention that she survive. They would be quick if she started to scream. She could tell that. Her only hope was to dive out the third floor window and take her chances. Breaking a leg or two would be better than what these two punks had in store for her.

Ben, the one still standing between Libby and the door, laughed out loud. The knife dangled by his side like something he was barely aware of, like he didn't really need it to do what he wanted to do.

Mack, though, gripped his knife with white

knuckles. He rocked from one foot to the other. "You get AIDS if you fuck'em up the ass, Ben? Can you still get AIDS from that?"

"Don't be a dumb ass. She's lying. She don't have AIDS. She's a liar."

She wanted to ask them if they were really willing to take that risk but she was losing her nerve. All she could think about was that open window. It was just across the room. She started to run for it. In a mere two steps, Ben tackled her and started dragging her to the bedroom.

*

Race six wasn't Frankie's race either. If he kept changing strategy, surely he would hit on the right one sooner or later. This time, he would go back to Window 6, to the guy in the plaid shirt and shimmery tie. He would buy the tickets for the last two races at one time. And, here was the clincher: he'd ask a total stranger, someone who looked lucky, for the names of horses to bet on. A beautiful woman is always lucky he figured. Someone beautiful is born lucky. There was a woman standing at the rail, a tall brunette in her twenties, thirty max. People didn't dress up to come to the races, but this woman was dressed like she was going to a White House dinner. She wore red high-heeled shoes and a black dress that bared one shoulder. A thoroughbred for sure. Lady luck for sure. What was she doing standing alone?

Frankie took the steps two at a time until he reached her.

"You look like a lucky lady," he told her. "Maybe you can help me out. You got favorites for the last two races?"

She looked him over. Smiled.

This has got to be it. Frankie could feel himself getting erect and he dropped his racing form down to cover himself.

"I'm not a betting girl myself," she said sweetly. "But my boyfriend has a horse in each race. Why don't you bet on those?"

"And what are those horses, lucky lady?"

"It's Dark Passion in the seventh and Lucky Legs in the eighth." She watched him; he didn't mark his racing form but repeated what she told him. When she turned and walked away, Frankie heard her say over her shoulder, "They're sure things." He was almost positive that's what she said.

Watching her walk away like that, the way elegant women walk in high heels, as though the swaying hips are keeping them in fluid balance like a yacht on water, he couldn't help but think of Libby and how she hated high heels. Still, Libby was beautiful and he loved her and every fight they ever had, he was sure, he was almost sure, was about getting married and having a baby. It wasn't his gambling per se that she objected to but the notion that a gambling man was never home. She didn't want to raise kids with a father who spent all his time at the track. Tonight's fight was a doozey. She'd warned him three months ago that he had to join gambler's anonymous if they were going to stay together and he appeased her by saying he would. He wasn't addicted to gambling, though; he just liked it. He liked the stale beer smell near the ticket windows. He liked the awful stench of the men's room. He liked the fresh air and the horses, the bright colors of the jockeys' silks, and the pounding of the hooves. He liked everything about the track the way Libby liked Macy's. He didn't see the difference. The battle had been over his going out again and even though he told her he was going to play darts at Jerry's, she knew he was going to the track. He insisted he was going to Jerry's. "Call him if you don't believe me," he'd said pushing his phone toward her. "Call him and ask him. It's dart night at Jerry's." Frankie knew, though, that the real problem was that Libby wanted a ring and a family. He wanted that too, just not yet.

Frankie didn't talk to the guy at Window 6. He pushed his money through, "Dark Passion in the seventh and Lucky Legs in the eighth. Both to show." This time, for sure, it was a sure thing.

*

Ben ran his knife up Libby's t-shirt and threw her on the bed. "Give us some privacy, will ya, Mack?"

Mack backed out of the room and closed the door. Through the door he yelled, "Remember you promised! Don't fuck her up, Benny! Give me a chance too. Don't go back on your word!"

Ben didn't answer him.

Libby thought she was going to die of fright before either of them could fuck her up. She didn't know if she even wanted to keep her wits about her. She tried to remember what the true crime shows said, the ones like *Live to Tell* where the victim survived against all odds. Maybe she could get to the floor lamp and hit Ben with it, swinging it like a bat, aiming for his head. He was quick, she already knew that, and strong. She rolled over to try to scramble away on her knees, reach the lamp somehow, try to knock him out. He was trying to pull her shorts off but they wouldn't come off without taking the zipper down. Libby didn't realize she'd begun to scream, scream louder than she knew she was capable of.

"Look, bitch, I'll kill you then fuck you. It don't matter none to me which comes first."

She was on her feet. She grabbed the lamp and began to swing it wildly. She was in the corner of the room, swinging the floor lamp with all her might. Still, Ben was somehow next to her and she felt the knife go in and her knees buckle. Then again. Then again.

*

Then it was done. Over. He thought how lucky he was to have Libby waiting at home. She'd forgive him; she always did. It was a sure thing. When everything else had turned to shit, there was Libby. If she were a horse, he'd call her My Sure Thing. That was Libby.

Frankie got in his car and turned on the radio to easy listening. Frank Sinatra was singing "I did it myyyyyy way." Two Frankies. He didn't win a single race but he was still a lucky guy because he had Libby. And, he was going to do what she wanted, what he wanted too. It wasn't a big deal to stop going to the track. Oh, he liked it, that was for sure, but he loved Libby and he wanted to make her happy. He wondered how many times he thought this as he drove away after the last race. This time, though, he meant it; the last race would be the last race.

He didn't see his clothes strewn across the lawn. He'd come in the front way and his clothes were scattered across the interior courtyard. He was practically whistling up the stairs thinking about proposing to her, well, maybe not proposing, more promising to propose, when he saw the open door. The apartment had been ransacked and his first thought was that she'd trashed the place and gone, that the fight that night had been the last straw for her. The window was open; could she have jumped out the window? Would she do that? He looked out to find his clothes, light, colorful patches on the black lawn, some shirts floating on the pool, some at the bottom like bright, undulating fish. She must have been pretty mad, he thought, and tried to think where she would have gone. Not far, he was sure, and they could mend it. No problem. He loved her and she loved him. They could mend it.

He surveyed the room, his hands on his hips.

Whew, what a wreck! Then, he spotted his Ray Charles, which had slid out of its sleeve, and cracked as though she'd stomped on it. No! She did not! She couldn't! She wouldn't! He stooped down to pick it up, holding out his hands as though the record were a gunned-down kitten. Was that blood on the carpet? Four or five tiny red drops? It looked like blood. My god, is that blood on the wall? He was still half-crouched, rising up slowly as it dawned on him that something awful had happened here. He couldn't move, but he had to move. He heard the terrifying approach of sirens. This blood couldn't be her blood, but it had to be her blood. The police cars screeched to a stop, doors slammed, boots on the pavement. He craned his neck looking past the living room, past the hall, and into the bedroom. The bed was rumpled but Libby wasn't on it; the lamp was missing. Frankie heard the policemen pounding up the stairs sounding like horses on a track. He sank to the floor and sat holding Ray Charles while the police flooded into the house. Two of them stopped and stood near him, while others, guns drawn, made their way into the bedroom.

"Clear!" one shouted. Then, he holstered his gun and called for a crime scene unit and the coroner.

"Is she there?" Frankie's lips moved but he managed only a whisper. Then, without thinking, without volition, for no reason that he could think of except that it had come into his mind, had come, he supposed, to ward off the reality of what was about to happen, of what he was about to see, Frankie thought only of Window 6, of the guy in his plaid shirt and his shimmery green tie, and the beautiful woman in the black dress and red shoes.

36 Views of X

X always appeared to be keeping a secret — not someone else's secret but one that was hers alone. Maybe it was her smile, small and perpetual, that gave the impression of something hidden, as though her mind were always on something pleasurable and unspeakable, something she desperately wanted to share but couldn't because it would disappear in the sharing. I was watching her across the room; it was a faculty thing -- you know the kind: cheese, crackers, cheap wine. We'd gathered in Morgan Lounge and I was sitting on one of the dilapidated couches while she stood near the table where a grad student was dispensing wine into clear plastic cups. I took my eyes off her only for a split second, and when I looked back, she had disappeared—it was like desire itself had left the room.

X was one of the faculty wives—no, that's not quite accurate. She wasn't just any faculty wife; she was the wife of Allen Banning. I'd seen her before. It was one of those marriages that all associate professors dream of someday: an aging professor on the cusp of retirement falls for an adoring student and captures her with his grumpy and paltry fame, his status as a campus icon, his occasional speaking engagement in some romantic place like Lucerne or Paris. As an as-yet-untenured junior faculty member, I could only imagine having achieved the lofty ideal of procuring a trophy wife.

Her husband, Dr. Allen Banning, had contracted polio when he was twelve. His life and work were well-documented with a number of scholarly biographies and analyses so everyone who cared to know the details of not only his bedeviled childhood but that of his parents as well could find the material in the campus bookstore, library archives, or one of several websites devoted to him. The polio had left him with a severe limp and reliance on a leg brace and a metal crutch on his forearm. It didn't seem to deter the ladies who gathered around him to hear stories of his friendships with famous poets and novelists or listen to his tales of his stint with the Hollywood jet set when a book he'd written was adapted to a movie. We poor sap men struggle for achievement so that a beautiful woman will possibly come to adore us, but women are different. A woman seeks only that in a man, Achievement with a capital A. His looks matter less and, with some women, even the money is of little, but not of no, consequence. A woman like X is attracted to the power of her man's intellect in a way that we men can't completely understand. The beauty of a man's wife is directly correlated to his achievements. Professor Banning had achieved that status that we associate professors refer to as being well-armed. We meant that he had a beautiful woman on his arm.

    Last year, X, short for Xavia, very short, was still in the group of women who hovered around her famous husband even though she and Banning had been married three years by then. But this year, X walked, disenchanted, around the fringes of the room, stopping at the wine table, looking out of the beveled windows onto the quad, sometimes leaving to smoke a cigarette outside Rudner Hall. Banning didn't seem to be keeping a close eye on her as he had in previous years. It used to be the case that if someone stopped to talk to X, Banning would interrupt whatever conversation he was engaged in and join that of X and whoever dared speak to her.

Now, at the sound of Banning's voice, the co-eds leaned in. On occasions like these, he traded his crutch for a more dapper cane, which he rested between his legs, making the cane look very much like a rigid extension of his penis.

I stirred, got up as casually as I could, and sauntered out the swinging double doors of Morgan Lounge, down the stairs, and out to the smoking area. She wasn't there. I didn't smoke so I turned to go when X stepped out of a shadow.

"Get's stuffy in there." Her voice seemed deeper than I remembered, more Lauren Bacall than Audrey Hepburn.

I'm not a stammering kind of guy, but I felt shuffling and a little bit aw-shucks being caught following her. I managed a smile. "Yes," I choked out, "I needed some air myself."

I don't think I'd said that much to her ever, or she to me, and I was a blank about where this conversation might go.

"I'm Xavia," she said extending her right hand and drawing her left hand, the one holding the cigarette, behind her as if to shield me from the smoke. "People call me X."

It took me a minute to stop looking at her gorgeous face and realize she'd extended her hand and I took it gladly. Our hands didn't move. I mean that our clasping hands didn't result in a handshake; we didn't pump as though we were sealing a deal. We just stood there for a minute clasping hands. I didn't want to let go—her cool dry palm smack up against my sweaty one.

That wasn't good. It was fabulous, but it wasn't good. Every person knew or at least suspected (it was the English Department, after all) that beauty and sorrow were two sides of a very thin coin. Beauty and sorrow were like twins conjoined at the back of their heads and sharing a brain. But it wasn't sorrow I felt, at least not yet, it was fear, exciting fear.

"Boyd," I told her as she extracted her hand. I was wishing that my name had been something worth commenting on like Barak Obama, a name that would start a conversation. She turned her head to blow her smoke away from me but I wish she hadn't. I wish she had covered me from head to toe with her glorious Virginia Slim exhalation.

"Boyd? Should I call you Boyd? Is that your given name? Or is that your family name?" She had dropped her cigarette to the ground and twisted it into the cobblestones with her remarkable high-heeled foot.

"First," I told X, "Boyd Dixon."

There is something I should tell you. I had started out pre-law and actually finished law school and done some teaching. For three semesters, I taught the graduate course in legal ethics. During much of the course, we discussed the difference between morally right and wrong as opposed to legally right or wrong. We talked about intention and ignorance. We talked about compulsion and rage. We bandied about phrases like "should reasonably have been expected to know," "could have reasonably assumed," and "no intention to do harm." We talked about how philosophical ethics differed from legal ethics, about how philosophical ethics had to do with morality and not legality while legal ethics had to do with the law and not with morality. A lot of what was legal seemed a far cry from what was moral.

I never took the bar exam. While my classmates formed study groups and then dispersed to qualify to practice law in their preferred state, I stayed on as a barista in the local Starbucks and thought about what to do next. My family, of course, felt my path was clear: return to Kansas City where I would pass the exam to practice law at the Kansas State Bar. After ethics, though, that just couldn't happen. I'd thought law was about fairness and justice, but it wasn't. I thought it was about guilt and innocence, but it wasn't about that either. Practicing law is like playing a game of chess in which the pawns are real people. The law is about strategy. I wanted a kinder and gentler life than that; I applied to graduate school in Literature, earning first a master's degree, then a doctorate, and took a teaching position at a small liberal arts college in Vermont. That's where I am now…Vermont. Literature soothed my soul with its justice. Literature was more human, more forgiving. There is no romance in the law. You need to know this about me for what happened to make sense.

"Well, Boyd," her voice rippled through me like honey in hot tea, "I guess we should go back in."

That was how we met; that was how it began. When I got home that night, I sat at my desk, the stark light a beacon in my dark apartment, writing the first poem I'd written in years. I saw again in my mind her languid movements, glistening and sensual; she moved like a string of pearls, silently and with such grace that I knew it was the closest I'd come to ecstasy. And I saw again her bending to Banning's ear, whispering, her hand on his shoulder, then, a brief kiss to his temple. He had barely looked up.

For weeks, I admit, I stalked her. Got her habits down. The days she went to the coffee shop in the morning, the days she jogged through the park, the days she shopped at Whole Foods. Then, I schemed to meet her "by chance," arriving at the coffee shop a little before she did, waving her over to a table by the window.

"Please, sit." I was more comfortable now. I felt like I knew her, knew all about her.

"I haven't seen you here before," she said hanging her handbag by its strap around the back of her chair and taking off her sweater. "Boyd Dixon, right?"

"You remembered!"

I felt awkward, responsible for a good conversation, but X seemed content to look into her coffee, stirring slowly until the milk had all blended. Of course, I wanted to ask her about Banning, how they'd met, what had won her over, but that's probably what most people did. Expecting to be alone, she'd brought a book.

"What are you reading?" I asked her.

I don't remember anymore what it was—some low-brow mystery that Banning would no doubt have been embarrassed by. But I smiled and feigned interest just to keep her sitting across from me looking at me with those enormous brown eyes and that little mouth that always seemed to be on the verge of smiling. I'm not sure what she said, but I remember thinking how simple it would be, really…being in love with a married woman. It sounds complicated, but it isn't. I firmly believe that love ought to be simple. When love becomes complex, it ceases in some way to be love at all, if you know what I mean. It's easy to say that you love someone, leave it at that and be perfectly happy. Things get complicated when you try to say that you love someone because of this or that. It's cute at first. I love you because you snort when you laugh. I love that about you. Or I love you because you cry after we have sex. It starts simple enough, but then it progresses to I love you because I can always count on you or because you're always there for me, or because I feel safe with you. Then, things get complicated.

Then, "I love you because…" turns into "I love you but…" and that's when the trouble starts. "I love you but…" is the kiss of death.

It became our ritual to meet at the coffee shop.

After three times, we depended on each other to be there. After four times, our conversations became more intimate.

"Oh, I love Allen, don't get me wrong, but you can't really be a wife to a man like that."

I looked at her quizzically, "I don't understand. What do you mean?" This was tricky because I didn't want to turn into a girlfriend; I wanted to turn into her confidant. Sharing a confidence, hopefully, would turn into having a shared secret.

"Obviously, Allen is much older than I am."

I put my hand over hers, but she withdrew it without so much as a change in expression. She said nothing about it and I said nothing. I leaned back in my chair never taking my sympathetic gaze off her face.

But several coffee shop visits later, I put my hand over hers and she did not withdraw it.

"I married Allen's brains, not his body." She looked down into her half-empty cup. "I thought that would be enough. I wanted to be part of that interesting life he led, friends with his friends, his prestige would be my prestige." X sighed. "I found out it doesn't work that way. I'm Allen's muse and his handmaid. That's not the same as being a wife. I'm not really a wife."

This was a critical opportunity and I had to choose my words carefully. If this wasn't an invitation for me to make a move on her, I don't know what would be. She wanted someone to treat her like the beautiful woman she was. She wanted romantic love. I was sure I was right.

"Allen enjoys the adoration of women," she said, "but his childhood illness is catching up with him. He's not really capable of…" She stopped there. "Oh! I've said too much! I didn't mean…" She started to gather her things.

I held her arm, stopping her. "I've been writing poetry about you. Did you guess?" She sat down again. "You really are a muse, X, you are my muse too. But, oh, my god, you are so much more. It's been so hard not to tell you how I feel. I'm embarrassed and ashamed." Here I hung my head. Then, head still bowed, I cast my eyes up, "Could you possibly think of me that way at all?" I gave her a little space to respond. When she didn't, I went on, "I hadn't written anything since the brutality of my doctoral thesis but you inspired me and I found myself writing poetry like I've never written before."

X sat stone still. I could read her mind. She was thinking it over. She knew we had come to a moment of truth. Would she or wouldn't she?

There was some new heat in her body that I could feel across the table.

"Would you like to come see my poetry?" I had broken out in a sweat.

Yes, she would.

X wasn't a disappointment. She was as beautiful without the elegant trappings of her clothes as she was in them. Her silky, blue undergarments made me wonder if she'd anticipated that today might be the day. Still, a woman like her? Maybe she always swaddled herself in beauty and luxury. Poor Banning! To lose his powers just when he'd procured this lovely creature! I had to smile at his misfortune.

"What's making you smile like that," X asked playfully.

She'd caught me. "Oh, the extreme, ecstatic pleasure of this moment." I meant that. I ran my hand down the creamy skin of her naked torso.

Immediately after she left the first time, I fell back into my crumpled bed to absorb the warmth and scent that lingered there, smiling like a complete moron, and then, unexpectedly with shocking rapidity, being absolutely overwhelmed by guilt. Damn that ethics course! I didn't use words like morality, sin, or adultery…I used words like intention and culpability. I went over the mitigating circumstances.

We began meeting exclusively in my apartment. After several weeks, X said, "You know, Boyd, I love you because you don't try to show me off like Allen does. I'm not just a prize to you."

I froze. She had skipped the cute stuff and gone right to the hard-core obligations, pinning me down to a kind of behavior that I didn't necessarily want to commit to.

"I'd love to show you off, my beautiful X," I told her, "but showing you off would end us. You're like a stolen work of art that I must keep hidden to enjoy."

It was a mistake, I know, to compare her to an object, but that didn't occur to me until she'd gone. The horrendous thing was that X was successfully serving as my muse. I wrote like a madman, one poem after another, a series I called "36 Views of X," and they were quite good. I wanted to send them to a publisher but how could I? I was reluctant to change the title because it was so perfect—"36 Views of Debbie" simply didn't have the same resonance. Each time X left, I was haunted by guilt and self-loathing and yet I couldn't stop myself. I was doing a terrible thing. I was being the kind of guy I hated. My attitude and interaction with Allen Banning changed, of course. I emanated a smirking attitude, I guess you'd say. Where I had been the male equivalent of the young female grad students who gathered around him, now I showed little respect for him, which isn't to say I didn't respect his work. I did. At the same time, every time I greeted him, I had to restrain myself from blurting out, "I'm bonking your wife." It was a kind of one-upsmanship. But, as my work was improving thanks to his muse, his work was diminishing. His latest novel met with mediocre reviews. His sales were good because he had his fans but he had hit his expiration date. He was definitely physically and mentally on the decline.

Perhaps, Allen Banning was in a steeper decline that I had imagined, yes, or maybe even hoped. He went into the hospital, the muscles of his body failing, even his heart muscle. Polio is an insidious disease and doctors able to treat it have long since retired. It is a disease that no longer exists. Ten days after he was admitted to the hospital, he was dead.

I saw X very little in those ten days. I didn't call her, of course, because she was busy tending to her dying husband. No, that's not the total truth. The reason I didn't call her was that I felt hollowed out myself. I mean, my chest felt empty as though my beating heart had been abandoned by the blood that filled it. I felt as though my heart, which had swelled with the music of X, was now deflated. I went to the funeral and there she was, her statuesque thinness seemed bent and withered, her glowing skin a sallow, waxy yellow, her eyes dull. The black she wore so often had become, not the sophisticated black of the wife of a brilliant professor, but a somber widow's black, the black of someone who had suffered loss, who had aged prematurely from grief, who had fallen some how from the grace she enjoyed as Allen Banning's wife. Watching her, I felt no lust for her. I felt nothing at all for her. As the condolence line made its way, one mourner by one, to her bereft hands, I slipped away.

I told myself I was letting sufficient time pass after the funeral before calling her, but the ruse was thin and I saw through my own excuse. She was of no interest to me; she was not Allen Banning's wife anymore. She didn't call me either, not for a long time. I had sunk myself into reading everything Banning had written. The semester passed with Banning's ghost lurking in the shadows of Morgan Lounge and palpably lingering in his old office. His death had thrown a pall over faculty get-togethers. It was left to the department secretary to pack up Banning's office and forward the boxes to his widow.

Toward the end of the semester, X did call, but I didn't answer. I picked up my phone to find out who was calling and when her name appeared, I simply stared vacantly at the phone waiting for it to stop ringing. She left no message. If our adulterous affair gave me moral angst, there was more angst in the knowledge that the affair had never been about X. I felt devastating shame over that. I realized that X was like Banning's surrogate; I wanted Allen Banning to care about me, to approve of me, and when X cared about me and approved of me, it felt like the same thing. What a cruel trick I'd played, on her and on myself! It was made crueler still for not apologizing or at least explaining. I didn't want to know if her loss of Allen Banning was made worse by her loss of me or if that was sheer hubris on my part. Was she collateral damage that I had created? Was her sorrow the unintended consequences of my confused obsession with her? I could be satisfied with neither a yes nor a no in answer to those questions.

X left the house they'd lived in and the town where he'd taught. She went somewhere else. I don't know where. I don't want to know.

Three years after Banning died, "36 Views of X" was published and although not at the top of the best seller list (what book of poetry ever is!), it was the best selling poetry book of that year. I often think of the first line that was generated the first time I laid eyes on X: In the beginning was the word and the word was desire and all things sprang from it.

But the desire, the desire I directed toward her, was a desire to have what Allen Banning had. I'll never have that. I know that now.

Maurissa takes the F-Scale

The California F-Scale was designed in 1947 by Theodore Adorno and others. It is a personality test devised to detect Fascist Tendencies.

Question Sixty-Seven

When you come right down to it, it's human nature never to do anything without an eye to one's own profit.

The room is too warm and Maurissa is feeling not only thirsty but oppressed. Her boss, Paul Kohler, chose the small conference room the firm had rented across from their main office in order for the staff to take the survey with as much privacy as could be managed. An outside administrator had been hired to monitor the survey. Maurissa chews gently on the eraser of her number two pencil wondering how she is supposed to answer these questions. She is angry at Paul for making her do this, angry at him for lumping her in with his anonymous staff. The questions are ridiculous really. What's the point? She's almost finished and glances first at her watch, then at the end of the test. She sighs. She re-reads Question 67: When you come right down to it, it's human nature never to do anything without an eye to one's own profit.

What is corporate hoping to find out with a question like that?

Maurissa considers the question. Human nature?

Paul said that her raise would definitely NOT depend on the results of this test but Maurissa doesn't trust him. She knows Paul better than that. Why spend the time and resources if it means nothing? She searches her memory for examples that she thinks demonstrate the general characteristics of human nature. Well, there is Paul and what happened yesterday afternoon.

Maurissa's phone rang a little after noon and

she had gotten up from her bed after their weekly tryst to fetch her cell from the living room. She had come back into the room frowning. Still naked, Maurissa crossed the room while Paul followed her with his eyes. She tilted the blinds open letting in the afternoon sun.

"Something wrong?" Paul asked. "Maurissa? Who was on the phone? Was it bad news?" He propped himself up on his elbow, the sheet casually falling away.

"Bad news? I don't know." Maurissa was thoughtful. She pulled on a tattered red silk kimono. "Yes, I suppose it was bad news."

"What's that supposed to mean?" Paul was always a little cranky after lunch hour sex. "Don't you know bad news when you hear it, kiddo?"

"I wish I could think of a tactful way to say this, but I can't so I guess I'll just say it. It was your wife."

"Gloria?" Paul swung his legs to the floor and sat up. Maurissa sat down on the other side of the bed turning so that she more or less faced his back.

"How'd she get your number? What'd she say?"

"She said to tell you that she's taking an overdose and if you plan to see her alive again, you'd better be on your way home." Maurissa was casual, off hand, but Paul was panicked.

"Are you serious?"

Maurissa pursed her lips. Paul's clothes hung neatly over the valet she'd bought for him. Wrinkled suits after lunch were so obvious. Usually, he had time to shower before dressing again, still making it to work before the lunch hour was over. Maurissa went back to the office an hour after he did. But now, he just sat on the edge of the bed.

"Is she bluffing, Paul? Has she threatened before?"

"I don't know, kiddo. I mean, no, she's never done this before." Maurissa wasn't at all sure if his agitation was directed toward her, Gloria, or the situation. How had Gloria found out? How had Gloria gotten her number? Maurissa knew that Paul would hate the complication of so many unknowns. She could see him calculating whether he had been careless or whether Maurissa had.

"You've been married to her for fourteen years. Don't you know if she's the type to kill herself?"

"No." He ran both his hands through his thinning hair. "Is there a type? Be quiet so I can think, Maurissa!"

But Maurissa wouldn't be quiet. "Well,

obviously you don't think your wife is the type or you'd at least be putting on your pants."

"No, Maurissa, no, that's not even the right question…if she's capable or not. I can't say if she would or not. Anyway, that's not the issue." Paul hesitated a minute obviously trying to interpret Maurissa's stare. "Look, is she really being fair to *me*? I'm having an affair and it isn't the first. It's punishable by divorce but Gloria has no right to harass me. She thinks she can control what I do by threatening me? It's blackmail. That's what it amounts to, doesn't it? She's trying to manipulate me and that pisses me off."

This was the Paul Maurissa knew so well.

"I suppose that's a healthy attitude," she said.

Paul was up now, pacing back and forth, clasped hands resting on his bare butt. Maurissa imagined that was how he looked in his office trying to decide if he'd take a case; he had clothes on then, of course. He was younger than Maurissa by a few years but he looked older. His slightly curved spine accentuated his small paunch. There were depressions on the bridge of his nose from his glasses.

"Come now, Paul. You couldn't possibly believe she'd do it or you wouldn't hesitate a second."

He shrugged. "I would think you'd be glad if my wife disposed of herself. One obstacle out of the way, hey, kiddo? No ex-wife to contend with, no alimony to pay."

"Believe me, that's the furthest thing from my mind. You'll recall that I am an ex-wife myself and the bed we just fucked in was generously provided for us by alimony checks. Besides, we've never talked about marrying each other."

"You're going to tell me you never thought about it?"

"Why would I want to marry you, Paul?"

"Women want to get married. Don't ask me why that's so. It just is."

"Why are we talking about this now?" Maurissa stood up. "Listen to me. Your wife just called and said she's taking a fatal dose of Valium. If there's a chance she's telling the truth, don't you think you should go home?"

"If I give in to it this time, Maurissa, who knows what she'll do to control my life." His voice betrayed a distinctly masculine whine she'd heard before in Paul.

"Gloria, my dear Paul," Maurissa said, "has discovered that her husband is having an affair. Being sinned against doesn't require her martyrdom. As you just mentioned, the solution of choice is divorce. I find infidelity hardly worth taking a life over. There are ways to prevent her from controlling your life, if that's what worries you. Perhaps with encouragement, she'd settle for simple mortification of her own flesh."

"It's the principle, Maurissa."

"I'm calling an ambulance. What's your address?"

"Don't. I'm warning you, Maurissa! That would be a mistake. This is really none of your business. You're not even involved really. Make some coffee, will you? I'm taking a shower."

"I'm calling the police."

"Why do you want to meddle in this?" Paul was yelling over the noise of the shower.

"Moral obligation, I guess. Call me stupid. Some sense of not wanting to 'stand idly by.' Give me some credit. I'm at least involved to the extent of being the other woman."

Paul didn't answer. He had stepped into the shower and could no longer hear her. If she did call the police, she didn't know where to tell them to go. Her affair with Paul was only seven months old but she thought she knew him pretty well. Could he really be so unconcerned if he thought his wife was capable of committing suicide? If Gloria could do it, really do it, Maurissa thought,

Paul would be home in a flash. All this nonsense about Gloria blackmailing him, about principle! What hooey!

Of course, Maurissa knew Paul well enough to know that he wasn't capable of NOT taking Gloria's actions seriously, not her overdose, her meddling in his affairs. The thought crossed Maurissa's mind that maybe this was how Paul always ended affairs. It would certainly work to end this one. Maurissa didn't know Gloria's voice. Perhaps, it wasn't Gloria who called at all. Maybe it was Paul's mistress-in-waiting. Thinking that she was involved with a man who would take a threatened suicide lightly — it was unimaginable. No, it had to be a bad joke. A joke on her. Maurissa put down her phone. Besides, this wasn't the old days. What stretch of the imagination would hold her responsible for Gloria?

Maurissa looked down at the test paper. Is it human nature never to do anything without an eye to one's own profit? That was probably true. She marked "strongly agree."

Moving to Jupiter's Moons

"Is this trash or what?" Nina stands too close, making Genevieve blink. Stupid women like Nina, Genevieve thinks, middle-aged, dull, sloppy, incomprehensibly sexy, believe all old women are half-deaf. Besides, she stinks of tobacco; nicotine stains on her fingers are the same dingy yellow as her hair. The three women who make up The Lady Boxers are as alike as cigarette butts and Genevieve simply thinks of them as Nina One, Two, and Three. Genevieve's daughter, Madelyn, picked the Lady Boxers out of the phonebook.

Every day for a week, Genevieve asked Madelyn, "When do the Green Bay Packers get here?"

"Lady Boxers, Mom." Madelyn corrected patiently each time.

"Lady Boxers, Green Bay Packers, whatever. When are they coming?"

Now Nina One bends down to look Genevieve in the eyes. "Does this stuff stay or go?" she hisses at Genevieve who turns away.

If Genevieve had the strength, she would lift the walker over her head and slam it into Nina One, knocking her to the floor so that the offending woman would look up at her instead of down.

Nina One places a dresser drawer, the last to be fetched from the cellar storage unit, in front of Genevieve. The Lady Boxers wheezed all morning, shuffling up and down the back stairs, three flights from Genevieve's apartment to the back door, then out, around, and down another flight into the basement, grasping drawer after drawer and retracing their steps, setting each drawer before Genevieve for her instructions. This one holds scarves not worn since Kennedy was president, handkerchiefs with crocheted edges not used since the invention of Kleenex. Genevieve sees the silver edge of a picture frame barely visible beneath them. There are postcards, too, thick bundles of them. "Why do people save these things," she wonders aloud. "Everybody saves postcards, silly scraps of cardboard from people long dead," she mutters dropping them in the trash box without looking at them one last time.

Nina One shifts her weight to one hip and sighs. All The Lady Boxers wear pink sweatpants with a once white tee shirt with pink letters on the back advertising their company. Their logo is a pair of hanging pink boxing gloves.

"Give me a minute to look through it, will you?" Genevieve snaps.

Nina One turns and disappears through the back door of the apartment, which she leaves open letting in the cold air of the hallway, making Genevieve shiver. Genevieve hears Nina One hit each step all the way down the three flights; then she hears the outside door slam.

For a good minute, Genevieve sits looking at the scarves in her hand without really seeing them. They haven't been worn in forty years; yet, like someone paralyzed, she isn't sure what she should do with them. The logic she's used all these years to hang on to them suddenly seems ludicrous. There is never going to be a time when they "might come in handy." Never. There is never going to be a time when she will "think of something clever" to do with them.

Genevieve is no longer sentimental about these things, so she doesn't quite understand why parting with things that should have been thrown away years ago upsets her. She drops the scarves in the box destined for the thrift shop. This leaves the photograph in the silver frame exposed. Seeing the picture for the first time in so many years takes her breath away. It couldn't be more shocking if stage curtains opened to reveal the photograph or if an ocean wave receded to expose it. The blood drains out of her the minute she lays eyes on it. It is a portrait of her, her face as it hasn't been for a long time, looking slightly away from the camera.

The portrait makes her look snobbish, she thinks, the way her face turns away from the camera, not looking away in defiance or in shyness, but looking away like an emperor on an old Roman coin—an expression of offended nobility. Or maybe her head was half turned listening. Someone off stage. Out of the frame.

The Lady Boxers are coming to the end of emptying the apartment. Drawers and boxes from the darkest corners of Genevieve's life were dragged out, examined, disposed of. With each item, Genevieve passed judgment; this thing stays, this thing goes. Now, she picks up the photograph and wipes the silver frame on the hem of her dress. Dis-remembering had been painful, she thinks. It had taken time…many years. She had tucked the picture away, looking at it only on the anniversary of the occasion, eventually letting the anniversary slip by and finally, not looking at it at all, or hardly at all.

In the picture, it is Patterson's eyes she is avoiding. He took this picture of her. Patterson Durm. She was annoyed with him that day as she often was. Maybe what annoyed her was his fussing with the camera, setting it just so, talking to himself, sighing and clicking his tongue, taking and re-taking the picture as though he had the temperament of an artist, wiping the lens with his handkerchief. The truth was that Genevieve was perpetually annoyed with Patterson because he was beautiful…yes, he was beautiful. Not handsome. His hair was like a child's, white-blond that lay thick as raw silk threads. His nose was thin and his eyes bright blue, his hands too delicate for a man's. She hated loving someone so elegant.

Genevieve sets the photo on the table (that and her chair are the only furniture remaining in the room besides the boxes destined for storage and the thrift shop) and looks out of the tall, narrow, bare window into the street that changed over the years but still remains so much the same. There was always a deli although not the same deli and a cleaner and some shoemaker or another. On the corner is a small grocery store owned by the same family since Genevieve and her husband moved into the apartment almost fifty years ago.

In the photo, Genevieve's skin is the color of boredom. Her eyes look dull. She supposes she often looked that way when she was with Patterson even though she loved him. By the end of that day and even now, she struggles to forgive him.

The picture was taken in December. The world was all black and white. She remembered that she had taken off her woolen hat at his request and her gloves too so that her pale hand could rest on the winter-black tree. But...where was the vapor of her freezing breath? Where was the raccoon collar of the coat he'd bought her that Christmas? No, not December. It was early March, wasn't it? The trees were just beginning to come to life. It wasn't December at all. How well she dis-remembered. It was warmish for that time of year, and she and Patterson went out because of the beauty of the day, the relief it was from bitter February. And she remembered thinking that the harm of him came in gentle whispers like the teasing and unseasonably warm breeze of that day.

Nina Two's hand suddenly appeared at the edge of the photo. "Storage?" Nina Two's shirt is freshly stained with coffee.

"Don't touch it!" Genevieve says, panicked, as though the picture is suddenly hot. "You can see I'm looking at it, can't you?" Nina Two turns away without apology. Genevieve feels used to women like them. Sullen. Disrespectful. "And what's that you've got?" she calls after her.

"Just books," Nina Two's tone is matter-of-fact but her look challenges Genevieve.

"Humph! Just books she says!" Genevieve stretches out her hands as though to take them from Nina Two, but seeing her own hands in front of her, fragile, dry, brittle as Valentine roses in May, she knows she's already grown too old to bear their weight. "Set them on the table. I at least want to say goodbye to them."

Nina Two does as Genevieve asks but walks away muttering, "If you say goodbye to every damn thing in this dusty old place, it will take us another week to clear it all out."

Some of the books belonged to Charlie, of course, left un-minded for some twenty years without him to open them. The books, she thinks, aren't like his coat that hung until this week in the part of the closet that used to be his. The coat is Charlie's body, what she sees when she remembers the figure of him, the beautiful proportions of Charlie at twenty-five or even at forty. Yes, even at sixty. She smiles a little, picturing him with the collar of the coat turned up against the cold; the length of it falling just to meet the tips of his fingers and covering his precious rear-end: the navy color almost black to match his hair. It is the coat he'd worn every winter in the half-open dry cleaning truck he drove, picking up the soiled laundry, delivering the fresh. The books though, they are Charlie's mind. Many evenings, she and Charlie snuggled under the covers to keep warm in the cold apartment, reading favorite passages from these books. *Don Quixote*: how many times did they read that! Carlyle's *The French Revolution*. They'd pour wine and toast, "The king is dead. Long live the king" when Louie was beheaded.

What good are they, these books? It is Charlie who is out of print and the books belong to anybody with the good sense to open them. Why didn't she dispose of them a long time ago? She tosses the books into the thrift store box; one among them, though, a gift from Charlie, she retrieves, sets aside. Then, she picks up the books again and moves them to her storage pile.

When the front door rattles open, Genevieve knows it can only be Madelyn. She doesn't see her daughter immediately but she can hear her speak to what passes as the supervisor of the motley crew sent to disassemble Genevieve's life. Then, when she turns in the chair where she is sitting, Genevieve sees Madelyn standing in the hall where boxes are stacked to cart off to storage. It is the only way Genevieve would agree to go. Her things are *not* to be thrown out, *not* to be sold, and *not* be given away until she is finished with them, which she definitely is *not*! Not yet anyway. Her things must be kept in storage in case she needs them — wants them back. The apartment Genevieve is moving to is too small for the armoire that she begged Charlie for, too small for the silk-covered settee that they paid for over time. She can take only enough books to fill one wall of shelves, only enough china to fill the smallest of her cabinets. There is not enough wall for the seascapes and not enough floor for the rugs willed to them from Charlie's Aunt Maureen.

The three Boxers scurry around shoving the last items into boxes.

"Mother," Madelyn greets Genevieve, bending to kiss her cheek. She pulls up a crate to sit on. "How has the day been? Not too painful I hope." Madelyn sighs too much and sits down too heavily, Genevieve thinks.

Madelyn just celebrated her fiftieth birthday. Genevieve is not prepared to watch her only child grow older. But Madelyn is still youthful because she married well, never had to work hard, but is, as Charlie used to say even in Madelyn's younger days, well-tended.

Madelyn didn't want her mother to stay in the apartment during the move, didn't want her to watch. She asked her mother to pick out what she wanted shipped to Florida and follow it there soon after.

"But, how can I know what I want? This pair of shoes or that? These sets of sheets or those? The seascape or the landscape?" Genevieve argued, "I saw the place for two hours and I'm supposed to 'pick out a few things to take with me? How can I?"

At Jupiter's Moons, Madelyn smiled and nodded her head as the agent pointed out the safety features: an alarm next to the bed, another in the bathroom, and one in the kitchen. Grab bars, smoke alarms, carbon monoxide monitors, safety locks, panic buttons were all standard features. Wake up calls, room service, laundry service, taxi service all for an extra charge of course and wasn't Mrs. Jackson lucky to have such a generous son-in-law who had done so well?

"Painful? Well, Madelyn, there's no avoiding it." Genevieve knows that Madelyn and Ray are trying to do their best for her, but she also blames them for something she can't name. She pats her daughter's hand. "What better life to aspire to than a senior living condo in Jupiter, Florida, on the sixth floor of the up-scale Jupiter's Moons, each building named after a moon, mine being the beautiful Callisto building, with my apartment on the ocean side no less, like something from a Seinfeld episode."

"Honestly, Mom, I'm sorry this hurts you. I'm truly sorry."

"What's to be sorry? If I could, I would dance." Genevieve wiggles her walker back and forth to simulate a kind of frenzied waltz. "It isn't your fault, Madelyn." Genevieve, among other things, forgot to pay her bills and didn't realize it until the lights wouldn't go on and there wasn't any heat. She told Madelyn she didn't know whether to laugh or cry. She got her medications mixed up time and again and, more than once, she caught a frying pan on fire.

"Well, you won't have to worry anymore." Madelyn spies the photograph now resting in her mother's lap. "I've never seen this picture of you," Madelyn says picking up the photo. "Did Dad take this?"

No one had ever seen that picture except Charlie, not even Patterson. Time is running out for the telling of secrets, but this one? It is something Genevieve never talks about, never will talk about, partly because it is not possible to let the words escape into the air where she might have to breathe them forever.

"No," Genevieve says, "It wasn't your father but I can't really remember who might have taken it. It was a long time ago."

"How old were you?" It's a natural question but, to Genevieve, it feels like prying, like Madelyn is determined to get to the bottom of something.

"About twenty I think."

"The year you and Dad were married? But he didn't take it?" Madelyn persists.

"Maybe your father did take it," Genevieve lies. "Who can remember now?"

"Well, you look so pretty in this picture. So deep in thought."

Genevieve almost tells Madelyn just to take it. But then the photo would only be of Genevieve when she was twenty. It is much more than that.

Madelyn sets the picture down.

"Have you had any lunch?"

"How am I supposed to have had lunch? The movers took the refrigerator first thing. There isn't a crumb in the house. And I had to fight them not to take my bed!"

"They left the bed?" Madelyn cranes her neck to look through the bedroom door.

"Yes, they left the bed," Genevieve says triumphantly. "Where would I sleep if they'd taken it? As it is, I can't get anything to eat."

"You're coming home with me, Mom. Remember? Staying a few days until you're ready to take off for Florida? Your things will be all moved in by the time you get there. You really can't stay here tonight."

"I'm staying here. I still have a bed."

"We want you to stay with us." Madelyn emphasizes *want* to deny the more adamant *need*. "We won't be seeing you as often anymore."

Genevieve can tell it isn't what Madelyn intended to say. She knows Madelyn doesn't want to remind either of them, but there it is.

"What would you like to eat?" Madelyn looks

down at her hands that fiddle urgently with her cell. "I'm hungry. How about the deli? You won't get a deli like Adele's in Jupiter."

"No, no, how can I go? They'll have everything mixed up. Everything that is to be given to charity will end up in Florida and all my best rugs will be given to the thrift shop. You go. Bring something in."

Thinking of staying with Madelyn and Ray "a few days" already annoys Genevieve. She would see them again, but she would never again see the apartment on 153rd Street. Besides, Genevieve hates the suburbs. It is almost more than she can bear. Madelyn and Ray live across the river in New Jersey in a big house in a new neighborhood where they have to get in the car to go buy even a pint of cream. In the mornings there, no church bells ring and no horns honk and the only sound is the barking of dogs elated to be out in the morning air. Genevieve calls it nouveau common, but not to Madelyn's face. The lawns look as though they've been delivered from a florist's catalogue and, there it is, the lawn right outside the front door. Not the same at all as being three flights up. What's to keep the dirt from blowing right inside the house?

Madelyn gets up to go to Adele's. Genevieve

can see Madelyn's cell phone finger itching to call the movers to come back and take the bed as Madelyn told them to in the first place. And Genevieve can sense that *the talk* is not far away. Madelyn would repeat, as she had so often in recent weeks, how nice Florida is. How nice everybody is there. How she and the kids would come to visit at least three or four times a year and, between times, Calvin, Genevieve's nephew, would drop in. It isn't that her life is in this place. Her life was never anywhere but in her and in Charlie and in Madelyn. Now, in her grandchildren Ryan and Sara-Beth too. Descendants. Like a Slinky going down stairs. One generation falling into the next.

She would be alone with her thoughts then. In Jupiter. The apartment is on the ocean side of the building and there is a little balcony there — not large but big enough for a lunch table and a couple of chairs.

Genevieve suddenly realizes that the Lady Boxers must have gone out the door with Madelyn. It is normally so peaceful when she is alone, but now the memory of Patterson stirs her up, gets her thinking again about those times. Patterson was slender, and his slight build made him the target of brawny men like Charlie. But

Genevieve always thought that Patterson had an aristocratic look, as if his ancestors hung on a castle wall somewhere in England or Germany. Patterson had the pompous air of royalty far removed from the throne; Genevieve teased him calling him Patty, as though he were among the pub-crawling Irish. He took it not at all good-naturedly. He wasn't lovable, no, not by a long shot; he was gloomy and brooding and that's what may have attracted Genevieve in the first place. She felt as though she were the one ray of sunlight, casting her warmth on his pathetically dark soul, the only one who could warm his frigid, bruised heart. It's the curse of some women to desire the guy who needs them.

Adele's is just downstairs and it doesn't take Madelyn long to return with two bowls of soup and some knishes.

"I was just thinking, Madelyn, about what a good husband your father was."

Madelyn smiles setting the deli bags on the windowsill until she clears the table, setting the few remaining things back in the drawer on the floor, except for the photo which Genevieve tucks beside her in the chair. Madelyn pulls Genevieve's chair and a crate to the sides of the table and opens the bags, setting Genevieve's food in front of her.

"I had a good father. I miss him still." Charlie has been gone for twenty years. He barely retired when one day, he came in from the hot afternoon sun and complained of a headache; he simply went to lie down and never got up again. "What were you thinking about, Mom?"

"Oh, about what good care of me he's always taken. I mean, look," Genevieve sweeps her arms around to indicate the vacant apartment. "True, we never had much money. But he always planned for me. Planned that I'd be taken care of financially after he died." Madelyn smiles the whimsical smile of people spoken to of the long dead. "Your father, he never really needed me. Never needed anyone. He was the most self-sufficient man I ever knew." Genevieve looks out the window toward the dry cleaners across the street. Her neighbor, C.J. is just going in.

"He seemed that way, didn't he? But," Madelyn hesitates, "he needed you and he needed me too. He needed us to need him."

"Does Ray need you to need him?" Genevieve asks, suddenly cross.

"Ray? Good heavens, no." Madelyn laughs a little. "Ray isn't wired that way. He needs me all right, but not to need him. What he needs is someone trustworthy to raise his kids and to be the housekeeper, to rub his feet and plan his social life. He'd just as soon I never needed him! He needs me to nail down his non-working life — which is getting to be a bigger job the older he gets!"

"Yes, these days, a man needs a woman to make the world seem like a habitable place." These days, she thinks, as though it was ever any different than that. Her phone rings and Madelyn, still chewing, gets up from her chair and waves her hand to indicate that she really must take this call and then moves off into the kitchen.

Had Genevieve needed Patterson to need her? Is that what gave her the power in the relationship, a power that she relished, but never had with Charlie? Patterson needed her all right. But she had not suspected how he needed her, not until the day in March when they had gone out to the park, Patterson armed with his new camera. He seemed unusually moody. He was never cheerful. Not that he was especially ill-tempered, either, but only that he was, for the most part, morose. It was such a pretty day that he decided to take out the Pierce Arrow that rarely left its spot in the garage. Patterson wanted Genevieve to take pictures of him posed against the sparkling grill of the vintage car. Had he said anything about engagement pictures? She couldn't remember anymore.

She can hear Madelyn talking on the phone and then coming back through the swinging door flipping her phone shut and tucking it into her pocket. From the look on Madelyn's face, Genevieve suspects that the time for *the talk* has arrived.

"Mom, the movers have agreed to come back and take the rest of your furniture. I know you wanted to stay here one more night, but it's Friday and they're booked tomorrow. Your stuff needs to go in the truck at the back so they can put another load in front of yours. We need to get the stuff for Jupiter on the truck today. They'll be heading for Florida on Monday." Madeline studies Genevieve. "Then," Madelyn continues, "the thrift store and the storage people will come get their boxes on Tuesday." When Genevieve shows no reaction, Madelyn sits down and begins to eat again. "I'm sorry things aren't the way you want them to be, Mom. I don't want to make this harder than it already is, but if we can just get through this, I know you're going to be so much happier in Florida."

Genevieve didn't seen C.J. cross the street

again but she knows the sound of his clomping on the stairs to the second floor, then to the third, and opening the door to his apartment across the hall.

"Mom?"

"Yes, I'm going to be happier in Florida. You've ordained it."

"We talked about this, didn't we? We said you don't have to go anywhere you don't want to go. You can stay right here in New York if you want to—just not in this apartment. Didn't we agree that you needed to be on the first floor or in an apartment with an elevator? You agreed that the change was a good one. The weather would allow you to be outside more and the services at the complex would be helpful to you? Didn't we agree?"

"Yes. We agreed. I'm sorry to be cranky. I'm sorry that this is difficult for me."

After a bit, the Lady Boxers come back, chatting, one still carrying a lunch bag from McDonald's. Genevieve can smell onions as the Ninas pass her. None of them look at or greet the two women for whom they work. Nina One, the supervisor, finishes a box she was working on before the lunch break, closes it, tapes it, marks it, and stacks it in the hallway with the others bound for storage.

Madelyn stands up and approaches Nina One. "What's left to do?" she asks her.

"Tape up some boxes. Not much. Get the trash out of here. That's about it."

"Would you mind stripping the bed? The movers will be back to take it. You can just leave the sheets on the floor in there."

"No problem."

"And, my mother's suitcases are in her bedroom. I think there are a few things in the closet. Will you pack them for her?"

"Sure."

"Along with any toiletries left in the bathroom?"

"Un-huh."

"If you don't mind, I'd like to settle up now. I need to pick up my son from a soccer game and I don't want you to have to wait for me to get back." Madelyn takes out her checkbook.

Genevieve finishes sorting the last drawer. Nina One, Two, and Three pick up everything but the photograph and the book Genevieve still holds onto. Everything else is packed in one of the boxes. The drawer is returned to the storage chest. The apartment is bare save for the chair Genevieve sits in and the round table. Madelyn settles up with Nina One and puts on her coat to leave.

"I hope to be back before the mover's come, Mom, but I'm not sure that I will be. We don't owe them any money until they get your stuff safely to Jupiter. Will you be all right until I get back?"

"All right? Of course I'll be all right. And if I'm not? What do you suggest I do?" Genevieve folds her hands across her stomach.

"I'll be back soon," Madelyn says closing the door behind her.

The Lady Boxers say good-bye and tell Genevieve that they will leave through the cellar door after they dispose of the trash.

There she sits. It is the first time she's seen this apartment empty in how many years? A long time. At the beginning of things. Madelyn was still a baby, barely walking, still in diapers. Now the place is empty again after fifty years.

Genevieve closes her eyes. She can smell, she is sure, the cherry tobacco that Charlie used in his pipe and suddenly she can smell, too, the pungent odor of a freshly fired gun. She'd only smelled that once in her life and it had nothing to do with this room — still, that part of her brain suddenly opens like a storage drawer spilling out its contents across her conscious mind.

Patterson's Pierce Arrow alone should have put Genevieve in an upbeat mood that day in

March. How perfect it was, how coddled. And Patterson's good mood too, but joyfulness expressed by Patterson got on her nerves. It was as if he had never mastered the art of happiness and threw himself about in awkward child-like poses and used his Donald Duck voice to make her laugh, which she adamantly refused to do. It was alarming when Patterson was joyful. When she had thoughts like that, she knew marriage to Patterson would be full of secrets. It was hard to account for the fact that she felt in love with him. It didn't make sense. Maybe it was just that Patterson's wife was a desirable person to be. Both his parents were dead, his mother of suicide and his father of cirrhosis. He had family money, went to the office when he felt in the mood, but the company was really run by a president and a board. He didn't seem demanding—no reason to be since the cooking and housekeeping were now and would continue to be done by hired help—and seemed, not only accepting but in fact encouraging of a degree of independence for his wife. And they loved each other, even though Genevieve, unsure that Patterson would ever propose, had let Charlie Jackson begin to court her.

They finished with the photos that day and

Patterson folded up the camera and put it in the floor of the backseat.

"I want to talk to you," Patterson said opening the door of the car for her. They always took off their shoes when he took out the Pierce Arrow and put them in felt bags kept in the car for that purpose. They rolled the windows down to let in the still warmish air of the day.

This was it, she thought. He's going to propose.

"I'm in love," he started. Somehow, to her shock, she knew instantly that Patterson wasn't talking about being in love with her.

"You're in love?" she stammered.

"Genny," he rarely called her by this diminutive. He turned her direction and took both of her hands, "I'm in love with Phillip." His eyes were riveted on Genevieve, monitoring her reaction.

She couldn't speak. It was 1950 and she had heard of homosexual men but she didn't realize, not only did she know one, she was expecting him to ask her to marry him. She knew that Patterson wanted her to look him in the eyes, but she kept looking down at his hands holding hers, his elegant hands with the meticulously buffed nails. She realized that her only reaction was a kind of speechless confusion.

"I didn't know if you suspected or not."

She felt as if she were choking. She felt as if, had she tried to utter a single word, something terrible would happen.

"Ask me anything!" he almost rhapsodized, "Really, I can't wait for you to meet Phillip! I adore him, Genny."

"Patterson, forgive me." She finally found her voice, but it was cracked with shock and uncertainty. "I'm really terribly confused."

"What is it, my love? I'll tell you anything you want to know."

"What are we doing together? What are you doing here with me?"

His face took on a gloom then that Genevieve was more familiar with. He put his arms around her as best he could in the front seat of the luxurious car. "Listen to me, Genny, I want you to marry me."

He had a tight grip on her and all she could do was blink into the highly-polished, hand-crafted dashboard. It wasn't that she expected this moment to be ecstatic, but she had expected it to be less complicated. Her mind was racing. It was impossible to sort out her thoughts and her brain went through a catalogue of who on earth she could talk to about this.

"I'd make a good husband, Genevieve." When he said her name, he always gave it the French pronunciation, Jon-vee-ev. " I'd provide a good life for you and you could take whatever lovers suited you."

Her vision of life as Mrs. Patterson Durm included shopping and volunteering and being respected for her graciousness as well as her wealth. At that moment, she tried to figure out a new vision, that, in reality, was not all that altered. Patterson, she realized, had never been part of the dream of marrying Patterson. It was marrying Patterson Durm she was in love with, not Patterson himself. Why shouldn't she live the life she dreamed of?

"What about Phillip?" Looking back on it, Genevieve knew the question was naïve. She should have understood what Patterson was suggesting.

He threw his head back and laughed. "No, no, my sweet! Phillip is mine. You can have lovers, but I won't share Phillip with you." He went from laughing to tears welling up in his eyes. "My life." He was addressing her. "You are my life. You will be my public life because you will be my public wife."

She sat stunned, watching as his tears twinkled in the fading light.

When she didn't say anything, he said, "I've taken a big risk, I suppose, revealing all this to you. I could have kept secrets from you forever. But, I know you love me and that I love you, and I thought maybe we could have everything we wanted. Women want a nice house, standing in society, money to spend—I can give you that."

She couldn't think. She couldn't quite absorb everything. That life she'd envisioned? Was it now only possible with a husband who…she didn't even know how to finish that sentence. Patterson loved her like a sister and she loved the life he could give her. That explained a whole lot. She'd thought Patterson only respectful, patient, if a little lacking in passion. She'd never even considered the life of a homosexual man.

She remembered thinking of the music room in his house, how the piano was never played. And how most of the bedrooms were never slept in. And how his real family was his servants and how she could change all that. She thought about her hands becoming as well manicured as his.

Genevieve is jolted out of her thoughts when the doorbell rings. It has gotten on towards dusk and there is no lamp to turn on. She has been sitting in the chair so long that she is stiff; getting up from the chair isn't easy. It has to be the movers coming back, she thinks.

"Just a minute," Genevieve calls, getting her walker into place and lifting herself up. The movers stream in and behind them is C.J. wiggling his eyebrows as though all moving men are irresistible. They let the movers pass on their way to the bedroom where they'd worked that morning. C.J. pulls a frown and then wraps her up in his hug, the walker between them like a chaperone.

"Going to miss you, Genny-girl." C.J.'s hug is one of the most sincere hugs she'd ever felt, but she almost collapses into his embrace. Genevieve's frail body sags into him and she can feel her legs giving way beneath her. C.J. leads her back to the chair and sits cross legged in front of her.

"You okay, Genny-girl?"

"I'm not so old, am I, C.J.?" She knows, of course, what the gentle C.J. will say. But it isn't her age so much as her brain that concerns her, memories flooding back to times that should have been long forgotten, forgetting things that happened only minutes before.

"You're one of those forever young types, Genny."

"I love you, C.J." Genevieve says thinking how easy that is to tell him and how hard it is with Madelyn or Ray. "I'm going to miss you."

"I'll come visit you. Send me a postcard with your new address. I'll come visit."

It all feels so awkward. Good-bye like that. Knowing he'll never really come to visit. Recalling that, for her, loss is becoming a way of life. He stays with her, watching the movers take the last sticks of furniture from the apartment.

One man returns with his clip-board. "What about that table and chair?" he asks.

"You want to come over to my place?" C.J. offers. "I've got a couch."

"You can take the table, but leave the chair," Genevieve instructs. "No, C.J., really, I just want to be alone for a minute." He gives her one last hug and follows the movers out.

It is absurd, her sitting there in the empty apartment, holding this photograph on her lap as though she were in the last scene of a movie when the screen fades to black and the credits begin to roll.

That night in 1950, she wasn't able to think quickly through the proposal Patterson made and she didn't get the time to think about it later. The sun was going down and it was already dim in the car. The air was chilly; they didn't think to roll up the windows, they were so rapt in each other. Patterson was facing her, "I do love you," he insisted. "We could have a wonderful life." His back was to the window and he didn't see Phillip coming up to them. Genevieve didn't know the man was Phillip. She had imagined a man who looked like Patterson, genteel, aristocratic, but Phillip looked more like a sailor. He was dark and stocky with bowed legs and wild hair that gave him the look of a gypsy. She thought at first he was just a man walking through the park but he came right up to Patterson's open window and grabbed Patterson's arm.

"What are you doing! Did you tell her! Well, did you!" Phillip screamed at him. Patterson was so taken by surprise by the sudden appearance of his lover that he, at first, fled across the car seat and up against Genevieve.

"Phillip?" he said, relaxing a bit, "What's going on? Why are you so angry? Calm down."

That did seem to calm Phillip down a bit. Patterson got out of the car and moved into the park with Phillip, moving to the tree where he had taken Genevieve's picture. She could hear them, barely being able to contain their voices, keeping them in shouted whispers, but she couldn't understand what they were saying. She didn't want to know. She just wanted to get out of there, to go home, to find a way to think. It was almost completely dark now. The lights were coming on throughout the park but the car was parked between two streetlights in a dark patch. Pretty soon, she saw Patterson striding back toward the car, his head down, intent on watching the grass pass with each long step. He came around and got in the car.

"I'm sorry about that," he said. "Lover's quarrel." He started up the engine. Just as he was about to pull away, though, Phillip came across the front of the car, rounding the beautiful fenders of the Pierce Arrow to reach Patterson, lifted his arm straight out like an infantry soldier, and shot once into Patterson hitting him square in the temple point blank. Patterson fell sideways into Genevieve's lap. She had never seen a gun before, never heard one, and at first no blood was apparent, but when she put her hand down to touch Patterson's face, she could feel the warm, thick, liquid just begin to well up from his temple.

"Be careful, Patterson, the car! Don't get that on the seats," and then she realized or somewhere in the confusion she must have realized. She couldn't help it. She slid across the soft calf seats smearing Patterson's blood that was beginning to saturate her dress. She opened the door and scrambled out of the car still in her bare feet. She didn't know whether Phillip would shoot again. She didn't know whether the single shot had killed Patterson. All she knew was that she needed to get out of the car. Non-sensically, she stood gaping at the open car door, at Patterson fallen over in the seat, at the blood dripping down into her handbag. Phillip was pacing in tight circles, banging himself on the forehead with his gun. He was groaning and crying as he paced and then he screamed out, shoved the barrel of the gun in his own mouth and shot once more. Genevieve shuddered and fell to the ground, overcome by the absolute horror of that moment.

Someone called the police. When they arrived, she was still collapsed on the ground, her teeth chattering, her body shaking with grief and shock. A policeman took a short statement. Someone handed her the camera and her blood-soaked handbag. No one handed her her shoes. A policeman drove her home in a police car.

What had possessed her to develop those pictures and to dispose of all the others but this one? The picture of Patterson, smiling, leaning up against his silver Pierce Arrow, his handkerchief dapperly peeking from his breast pocket—She couldn't bear, really, to look at it. And Charlie? Those pictures didn't need to be in the house. But this one of her just before this terrible thing happened? There's something about it, about her at that moment, as if it were the last time she were actually Genevieve Belouse—at least *that* Genevieve Belouse. It was before Patterson's dark shadow covered her forever.

For months after, she could barely eat or drink. All food seemed to remind her of Patterson's flesh, all drink reminded her of his blood. Charlie came over every day bringing her candy or flowers or books. And slowly, Genevieve came back to herself, her horror replaced by a deeply embedded pain that never quite left her.

She expected Ryan to be with Madelyn when she returned but she came through the door alone.

"Mom! For goodness sakes! Why don't you turn on the lights? Sitting there in the dark like that." Madelyn flips on the harsh ceiling light. "Did the movers come?"

"No reason to turn on the lights. There's nothing to see anymore."

"Did the movers come?" she asks again.

"Yes."

"They took the table too?"

"Yes."

Madelyn comes over and leans against the window sill. "Is there anything you want before we go?"

Genevieve can't answer. She reaches down into the chair she'd been sitting in all day and picks up the small volume she'd set aside when she went through the books. It is a five by seven edition of *Romeo and Juliet*, covered in Italian marbleized paper with gold leaf edged pages. Charlie gave it to her one year on their anniversary. It had become a habit to read to each other before they went to sleep. It wasn't because the apartment was cold that they did it really, but because they enjoyed their time together reading and talking to each other about what they'd read. This was one of their favorites. Sometimes, they'd do the balcony scene. Perhaps Charlie would have been fond of the idea of her moving to Jupiter.

"The kids are looking forward to us coming back for dinner, Mom. I told them I would pick up some of Adele's cream soda before we came home. She has that brand that nobody else seems to carry. They still associate that soda with visiting their grandmother. I never remember the name but I'll know the label when I see it." She looks steadily at Genevieve. "I had to park way down the street. Mom?"

Genevieve stirs then. Getting her walker into place, she raises herself up. She's left her purse on the kitchen counter and both the book and the photograph will easily fit into it. Nina One left the suitcase by the front door as she promised. Madelyn moves that direction and picks up the suitcase, at the same time looking at text messages on her cell. Genevieve glances around the apartment one last time, then on impulse, opens a kitchen drawer and places the photograph inside, closing the drawer again. She slips the book into her handbag. No need to take the picture, she thinks. It's better left behind. That's all over now. That's finally over.

"It's been a long day, huh Mom?" Madelyn says as she walks toward her. "But you're going to love Florida. Just wait and see."

Madelyn helps her mother down the stairs for the last time, holding the walker in one hand and her mother's hand in the other. They make their way to the car and Madelyn settles Genevieve in the passenger seat, folds the walker and puts it in the trunk. She heads to Adele's for the soda. As Genevieve sits there, panic begins to rise in her. Her brain begins to buzz. She left the photograph! Now she has nothing of that time — those moments before the terrible thing. What possessed her to do that? She has to go back.

It is dark; the streetlight is broken. Genevieve opens the car door and pulls herself out. She is wobbling back without her walker, steadying herself against the brick wall of her apartment building. She is just about back to her building when Madelyn comes rushing across the street.

"Mom! What are you doing? Where are you going?"

"I've left something. I have to get it." Genevieve wiggles her arm away from Madelyn and tries to go around her.

"There's nothing, Mom. It's empty. Everything is gone. What is it you think is there?"

"I have to go back and get it," Genevieve says frantically. "Let go of me, Madelyn, I have to go back."

"Tell me what it is, Mom, and I'll go get it. You don't need to climb those stairs. Let me take you back to the car, and I'll go get what you left."

"No," Genevieve says weakly as Madelyn turns her back toward the car. "No, I need to go myself. No one should touch…"

"What is it? I'll get it for you. What is it you think you left?"

What is it she left? It's impossible to tell. "Oh,

Madelyn," Genevieve mourns as her daughter helps her get into the car again. Madelyn is standing with the car door open.

"What is it? What do you want me to get?" She opens the back door of the car and sets the soda on the floor and closes the door again. "Mother? What is it you want? I don't mind going back to get it. Honestly."

When Genevieve doesn't answer, when she sits with her head hanging low, Madelyn closes the car door, goes around to the driver's side and gets in. She starts the engine and then glances over at Genevieve. "I'll tell Ray to check the apartment when he goes back for the sheets and the chair. If there's anything there, I'll send it to you. Okay? Okay, Mom?"

Madelyn looks over her shoulder, then pulls out onto the street. "Just think," she says, "in another week you'll be in Jupiter basking in the sun. You're going to love it. I just know you're going to love it."

Genevieve's chin quivers and reluctant tears wet her cheeks. She does not look back. The lights of the on-coming cars seem to turn night to day to night again. It is beginning to rain a little and Madelyn turns on the windshield wipers. Genevieve shifts in her seat for one last look at the apartment building that had been her life, but it is too late; the building has already disappeared. What happens next is unexpected. Genevieve suddenly feels lighter, feels as though some burden has lifted. She raises her drooping head to look at Madelyn but Madelyn stares at the road ahead. The next car that passes is like the rising sun and, in that rising sun, Genevieve sees the golden shore and bright blue sea from her balcony at Jupiter's Moons.

Jo Rousseau

Comrades

If I had gone straight down Seventh instead of turning left on Pine, if I'd started out on Wednesday when the meeting was originally set instead of Thursday when the meeting was rescheduled, if I hadn't missed the nine o'clock train forcing me to take the 9:15, I never would have come face to face with Joe Roth. I was absolutely dumb-founded, speechless at the sight of him. I stood there puzzling over the vast conspiracy of coincidence that put me in this moment. Joe Roth. Seeing him stopped me dead in my tracks. What was it? Twenty years? More? When I first got out of jail, I saw him everywhere I turned, in restaurants, in movie theaters. It was never him but some man, similar in looks, who set my heart on fire. But this was the real Joe Roth. He was unmistakable. Seeing him, I could once again feel his skin's warmth touching my skin, see him sleeping in the dim light that came through his tent with the morning sun. He had the same sandy hair that always seemed to be past due for a haircut, the same smooth skin that was way too good for a hockey player, and the same scuffed shoes—well, not exactly the same. The sneakers he wore then, even in the snow, had transformed into black leather, but not shiny, not polished, scuffed and a little worn. What was different was the crisp suit, the gray and blue striped tie, and the bright white shirt that made him look Wall Street from his shirt collar to the hem of his pressed pants.

Joe passed me without notice. I waited for him to turn; surely, he would somehow be intuitively aware of my presence, my siren call, but he didn't turn. He stopped at the coffee kiosk on the street in front of a busy office building. He stood examining a fist full of change, picking out quarters to hand to the vendor.

The last time I saw Joe I still carried my childhood nickname, Kiki. It was my second year at a small Mid-western college when he walked into my feminist literature class and took the seat next to me. Feminist literature was new in those days and he was the only male so every head turned when he entered the room. Between the civil rights movement and the war protests, the women's movement almost seemed like comic relief. Still, we'd made easy progress when schools began to enroll female students in almost all departments including architecture and engineering. There were no women's restrooms in those buildings, so female students had to go to the art school to use the bathroom but there was talk of converting the men's room on the second floor. Once we got the restrooms, more progress wouldn't be too far behind. Still, birth control pills were legal only for married women, abortion wasn't legal anywhere, and equal pay wasn't even on the radar because there were still so few women in the workforce, stewardesses, secretaries, waitresses being the exception. The women's movement was eclipsed by what everyone, even women in the feminist literature class, thought of as the life and death matters of racism and war. It was fall semester, 1969. Of course, it wasn't just our little campus that was in turmoil. Our whole country was teetering on the edge of chaos. We had been through a lot already:

John Kennedy, Bobby Kennedy, and Martin Luther King had all been assassinated; the signing of Lyndon Johnson's Civil Rights legislation in 1964 had changed things a little and now Black Power advocates were lobbying the universities for Black Studies classes; the Vietnam war that everyone thought was drawing to a close was heating up again. Richard Nixon had been elected in 1968 with a promise to end the war but, a year later, he revised the lottery draft system to eliminate student deferments. Every man we knew was at risk. The last time I saw Joe was the night of the lottery, December 1, 1969.

Rooms all over campus held anxious students, anxious sweethearts, anxious professors, all huddled together in lounges in math or English departments, in art studios or in the library meeting rooms. Joe and I took a seat on one of the couches in front of a TV in the law school lounge. Every couch and easy chair in the building was lined up theater-style to accommodate the three- or four-dozen people who gathered there. It was the end of the semester, finals week, but the campus population was in no mood to study.

I heard the girl in front of me whisper, "Robbie, turn out the lights. People will be crying."

The girl held Robbie's hand, not wanting to let him go, and then reluctantly let him go to do as she had asked.

"Where's Paul?" I squinted at the faces in the now darkened room.

"Studying, I guess. Says it's not going to change anything if he's not here and they call his number." Joe looked down at his feet as if they were in danger right then and there of being blown off. "He's right about that."

Joe and I didn't have the kind of relationship where I hovered over him. I didn't sit close or desperately clutch his hand or his arm like the girls we called bowheads because of the unserious ribbons they wore like elementary school girls. Sometimes, Joe called me "comrade" when we were naked in the tent that he'd set up in the quadrangle. I didn't mind. It made me feel like an equal; it made me feel strong. I wanted to be tough, wanted to be on the side of fighting to stop the war.

"He isn't going, is he? If they call his number?"

Joe shrugged. Maybe Paul was already over the border.

Most people had barely noticed when the military advisors in Vietnam turned into ground troops. Then, one day somebody says, hey, did you hear that so-and-so's brother was killed in Vietnam and you think, Vietnam? What's that? But by 1965, everybody knew somebody who knew somebody who was killed in the war that wasn't even really a war but only a conflict as if nobody ever died in a conflict. Every night, news footage made its way into living rooms across the country. In the early days, John Kennedy had banned the images of coffins being returned from Vietnam citing the privacy of the bereaved. The people believed John Kennedy. The people believed Tom Brokaw and Morley Safer and Dan Rather. And they believed Martin Luther King when he called on men to evade the draft. Trash barrel bonfires were held where young men threw away their draft cards or draft notices. But the war went on and on. Now, there were rumors that the war was expanding to Laos and Cambodia. War feeds on the blood of soldiers, and Nixon needed soldiers so he expanded the draft—no more college deferments.

The whispered conversations came to a halt and the room went as quiet as a body bag. On the television screen, three men in black suits and ties were in the foreground while a table of four or five men and women filled the background. It was a plain room with a curtain spread across the entire space in back of the people at the table and an American flag on the right of the screen. Each day of the year was assigned a number—366 numbers. The pieces of numbered paper were stuffed into plastic capsules and deposited into a jar. One man watched the numbers being drawn. One man drew the capsule out; one man opened the capsule and read the number. Everybody held a collective breath as the man in black opened the capsule and read number 258. Another man, checking his chart wrote, #1 September 14 on a blackboard. Those born on that day were the first to be called up. The one hundred and ninety-five numbers that would be drawn would make for a long, tense night. Girlfriends, faces streaked with tears, waited for each number to be translated into a calendar day. The crowd reacted to a near-miss, a dead-on, or a not-even-close number with a sigh or a cry. Some stomped out; others paced the back of the room.

Joe's number was called somewhere in the middle. He sat frozen for half a minute, got up, walked to the back of the room, walked back to me, sat down again, then got up, and walked out. After a few minutes, I followed him.

The war protests had been going on for four years with students taking a bigger and bigger role as dissenters. The quadrangle was now a tent city. The local campus group naming itself the SPU, Students for a Peaceful Union, was supplemented by representatives from the Students for a Democratic Society. Even though the Chancellor turned a blind eye when the non-protestors had to walk to class along pathways littered with cooking utensils, beer bottles, and amid the sweet smell of marijuana, the Board of Trustees was not so inclined. Most of the students picked up the trash as a way of doing their part for the cause or left cups of coffee or sacks of doughnuts or hamburgers to feed those willing to risk their future to protest the war.

The tension and anxiety leading up to the lottery ramped up the student protests. Joe was spending less and less time in his dorm room or in class and more and more time in the tent city established in the quadrangle. The liberal arts school was not inclined to call in the National Guard as had been done on some campuses around the country and no one disturbed the little community of dissidents as they set up tables to provide information about the war and the draft.

Joe and I relieved the tensions of the times in his tent, sharing a joint, sharing our bodies with each other, sharing our hopes and fears. I helped, manning the literature table, producing some of the literature myself, and in general being, not a protestor, but a protestor's assistant.

That December night, I caught up with Joe.

"Where you going?" I was breathless.

"To see Paul."

"What for?"

"We've got some business to take care of."

"What do you mean 'business'?"

Joe stopped. "Look, run along before you get in over your head."

"We're comrades, Joe." As hard as I tried to sound defiant, my voice was soft and beseeching.

"We *WERE* comrades. This is a new day."

As we passed the tent city, there were empty spots where some of the tents had already disappeared, occupants packed up, headed to Canada. Nobody knew how many numbers they'd get through in a year, but Joe wasn't going to sit around to find out. There had been word already of a kind of underground to a place in Canada where the draft-evaders had created their own special kind of illegal immigrant community. I suspected Joe planned on going there.

"Joe," my voice took on more steel, "this isn't about you. I want to stop this war just as much as you, and if you won't let me in, then I'll find another way."

He looked at me, bundled up in my white ski jacket with faux fur around the hood, "Come on, then," he said.

The truth was that I thought I couldn't stand it if Joe went off and I didn't know what happened to him or if I'd ever see him again. I admit even to day-dreaming a bit that if he went to Canada, maybe I would go too, live in the draft dodger community somewhere in the Canadian wilderness, maybe even in a tent just like in the quadrangle.

I waited in the first floor lounge for Joe to get Paul. The plan was to go to the Rathskeller, an on-campus student hang-out that served 3.2 beer. But, when Joe came down again, he was alone. He carried a note in his hand. Joe started walking and I followed.

"Where're we going?" I tugged on the strings of my hood pulling it tighter around my face.

"He's in Petry."

It was a short walk from the dorm to the student lounge in Petry Hall. When we got there, it was packed. How can I describe it? All eyes were on a short, stocky man who stood on one of the tables. His face was red and his sleeves were rolled up like a workman's. Sweat streamed from his hairline and he'd wipe it away with the back of his hand.

"Whoever told you that war was noble is feeding you a load of crap. Killing old women and children is not noble. Whoever told you there'd be heroes is lying. There's only the living and the dead. There's only those who come home breathing and those who come home in a body bag."

In the crowd, we saw faces of those who had left the law school lounge. Some of the faces were full of rage or crying, some of the fists were balled, ready to strike. The girls stood meekly by the side of their boyfriends. I did too.

"You going to give up your life for an illegal war? Sorry! Conflict!" he shouted from the table. "You going to spend your life with your legs shot off or your arms replaced by steel claws? For what? The Vietnamese haven't done anything to us. What's the fucking war about? Does anybody even know?"

More and more people joined the crowd, coming in after their number had been called or leaving in a huff after the tension got to be too much.

Tables were tossed aside to make room, people were standing on chairs to see the speaker or to yell out themselves.

Then, through the double doors of Petry Lounge came a group, no, a mob of men. I knew some of them. They were fraternity guys. They marched in tearing the attention away from the speaker.

"Hell no! We won't go!" they yelled in unison.

One in the mob climbed up on the table. Many in his group were pretty drunk, but the leader was stone sober. He chanted with them and soon the entire lounge was rocking with a thunderous roar. "We won't go! Hell, no! We won't go!"

The guy who had been standing on the table got down to make room for the new leader.

"We don't fight in Richard Nixon's profiteering war!" he shouted. "We don't fight in wars that don't draft senators' sons! We've given enough blood to that war. Vietnam is soaked in the blood of good American boys. It's time for this to stop!"

I don't know how long he went on before someone came in screaming, "The fucking ROTC bastards set the tents on fire!"

Petry emptied out in minutes to race to the site of the tent city. Boys took off their coats and started slamming them into the burning tents. Some took blankets or sleeping bags out of the tents that were not yet ablaze and used them to smother the flames. Quickly, the campus fire department took over.

There was such confusion, such racket, that I just wanted to find Joe and get out of there. But when I found Joe, he was already on a mission.

"Get out of here, Kiki! Go back to the dorm. I'll see you tomorrow," he told me.

No way was I going to do that.

"What's up? Where are we going?"

"Leave! This is no place for a woman."

Ms. Magazine was still several years in the future, but I was already steeped in Betty Freidan and Gloria Steinem. There was no such place as "no place for a woman."

"I'm going with you!" I had to jog to keep up with him. We were part of a small crowd and I had no idea where we were headed but the guys who'd stood on the table were leading us all somewhere.

"Where we going, Joe?"

He didn't answer me.

We half-ran across campus, across the football field, to a building on the other side that housed, not only the ROTC program, but the draft eligibility files of every male student on campus. Some of the students had picked up tent poles, some had gathered rocks along the way, and some had taken bricks from the flower gardens now covered over with mulch. One of the guys who'd stood on the table threw the first brick right through the window of the ROTC building. Two or three others rammed their tent poles into the window on the door until it shattered and then opened the door from the inside. I rushed in with the rest of them determined to do my part. At this point, honestly, Joe wasn't much on my mind. We were trashing the place and, it was not just joyous, it was exhilarating, exciting in a sexual way. I'd never felt that before and I wondered if that's how war felt, if that's how it felt to shoulder a rifle and blow somebody's head off. Our lovely little mob threw desk lamps out the windows into the parking lot; we threw trashcans and typewriters. Somebody pried open the file drawers and taking a match out of his pocket, set the contents on fire and then went to the next file drawer. Someone set fire to the supply cabinet full of paper and soon the whole building was in flames. I looked around for Joe. I didn't see him; everyone was getting out. The building was filling with smoke as office chair seats smoldered with a low flame and poured out lots and lots of smoke.

By the time I got out of the building, the police

were everywhere. The campus police had been joined by the city police and paddy wagons were already lined up ready to take us unpatriotic miscreants off to the station.

Seeing the police was like putting on your clothes after sleeping off an orgasm. The joy and excitement was replaced by disappointed low-grade panic. I had done the right thing. I had come down on the right side of history. It wasn't about Joe, I told myself. They shoved me into a paddy wagon along with eight or nine other people. We didn't speak—only one guy who sang the *Marseilles* in French at the top of his lungs.

I spent three months in jail. I missed my finals and was not let back in school. Joe had escaped somehow and I neither saw him nor heard from him—until today.

I had heard that Joe made it to Canada, to the wilderness where the never-to-be-veterans-of-any-war lived. I heard that from Paul when I called him and asked him to meet me at a coffee shop near campus. It had been finals week all those years ago and the campus library stayed open all night—even served coffee and pancakes in the library lobby. That's where Paul had been. Studying. He had never come to Petry, or if he had, he didn't stay. His number wasn't one of the

195 called that night. We kept in touch for a while but after a few months, Paul stopped hearing from Joe and there was no point. He said he thought Joe had met a woman, a Canadian woman, and thought he might marry her. He liked Canada. He thought it was more progressive than the United States.

The vendor was just handing Joe his coffee when he turned. I thought he looked straight at me, but his face, as far as I could tell, registered no recognition. I thought about accidently bumping into him, maybe spilling his coffee all over his spiffy blue suit, or following him to see if he worked in a nearby building. I thought about calling out, "Hey, Comrade!" so that he'd turn and maybe even smile, maybe be glad to see me.

Stories come to an end and our story had come to an end on December 1, 1969. There could be no sequel after all these years, no Part Two. But I wondered if he was happy, if he thought he'd made the right decision all those years ago, if he ever thought of me. I had stood long enough on the sidewalk to be late for my appointment. I'd let Joe pass me by and what rang in my head was, "Go home, Kiki, before you get in over your head." And, that's exactly what I'm going to do.

Love's Actuary

Jonathon Hartwell sat in Jake's Bar and Grill across from a pretty blond intently watching the glistening movement of her red lips. He'd stopped listening about three women ago and would be relieved when the remaining minute and a half elapsed and this woman would disappear to be replaced by another. He was doing his best not to look absolutely disinterested, plastering a smile on his face that he hoped did not make him look insane.

This wasn't his first stab at speed dating. He had done this the first Tuesday of every month for six months, targeting a woman to get to know better from each session. For the first two months, his selections left him with buyers' remorse, so on the third month he came up with a strategy that he hoped would net him the woman of his dreams. Certainly, Jake's offered a narrow sampling of women, and three minutes was hardly time to find his soul-mate, but Jonathon believed in a kind of fate that would place the right woman, of all the women in the universe, directly in his path, that is, sitting across from him in Jake's Bar and Grill. So, he refined his questioning so that it would almost serve as a code, a signal, that the woman across from him at this moment was the one woman, the right woman, the only woman with whom he could live a happy and peaceful life. Jonathon decided the most revealing question was: Do you own a gun? It was a brilliant question from which he could glean much information. A woman who owned a gun was a woman who looked after herself, who did not shrivel in the face of danger, and who understood her own strength. A gun-owning woman showed a measure of independence and a willingness to invest her time and money in creating the life she wanted to live. Most importantly, Jonathon wanted a woman who was willing to kill in order to protect herself, who had the confidence to value her own life over the life of anyone who threatened her. He soon learned, to his dismay, risk came with that question. Some women laughed in a way Jonathon found most unattractive and some looked frightened, no, downright terrified. Without doubt, some women, upon being asked his brilliant question, were sure the question was posed because the man across the table from her planned to lurk in the shadows of the parking lot after the session was over. The unsubtle question was intended to calculate his risk. And some women, he was sure, lied, looking him aggressively in the eye, and saying, "Own a gun? Right here, buddy," as she patted her handbag. But, overall, Jonathon felt the answer to his question was a solid indication of his perfect match.

Thus, having landed on the exact revealing question, Jonathon Hartwell, wisely and intentionally, devised his own scale, a variation on the traditional micromort calculator, one that would measure his own risk of death by the hands of his perspective life partner.

"Sadie," (this was the woman he'd selected in May), "do you shoot? Do you have your own gun?" He tried to be subtle, non-threatening, but he couldn't look her in the eye as he asked the question.

"Is shooting a hobby of yours? I have a friend who shoots. In fact, she and her husband manufacture their own bullets right in their basement. Sleeping right above all that gunpowder," Sadie giggled nervously, "would certainly not be my cup of tea."

Sadie rattled on, neither answering the question he'd asked nor letting him answer the question she'd asked. When the bell rang, Sadie dashed to the next table.

He assigned twenty-two micromorts, which would have offered him the same risk of death as the average person naturally encounters in the course of a day. That meant that Jonathon was no more likely to die at the hands of Sadie than he was to die of falling debris like an air conditioning unit that breaks free of its tethers. Sadie was as likely to run over him as any random driver traversing the streets of St. Louis. To be poisoned by Sadie was as likely as being poisoned by a total stranger. Sadie, to Jonathon's way of thinking, was average in every way.

The next day, Jonathon signed up as a member of The Range, a shooting club not far from Jake's. He wanted to be prepared to answer the question that Sadie had posed with a "yes" to calm fears of a stalker wanting to make sure the stalked was unarmed.

The month of June's fifty-five-micromort-Lisa had earned a significant number of additional micromorts because of her love of adventure. A criminal lawyer in a private law firm, Lisa relished skydiving and white-water rafting. To impress her, Jonathon had arranged a midnight, clandestine bungee jump and she, in turn, had taken him into the Ozarks one week-end to participate in a poisonous-snake-handling ritual offered by a local religious sect. Dating Lisa was death-defying in many ways and although Jonathon felt a certain exhilaration accompanied the time they spent together, he also felt in control, as if the danger offered up was a kind of commercial danger, an amusement park thrill ride into which many safe-guards were embedded. He could take precautions, he could back away, he could just say no, and if he had to, he could run like hell. But Lisa and the month of June came and went and by July he was back at the three-minute-dating table.

In July, he met Jean, beautiful, long-legged Jean who rated a little higher at sixty micromorts. It wasn't Jean per se that accounted for the addition of a few points over Sadie and Lisa, but it was Jean's context. Because she was beautiful, she had a number of suitors, some of whom, he suspected, were capable of jealous rages that might, intentionally or not, end badly for Jonathon. He was sure, for instance, that Jean's most recent ex, David Ludlow, was such a man. The topic of David Ludlow had come up on their third date in as many days. Jonathon had pulled up in front of Jean's row-house-style condo and there was David sitting on the top step of her front porch, smoking a cigarette, which he flipped away when he saw them. Instead of getting out of the car, instead of Jonathon walking Jean to her door, she asked him to drive away. That was on Friday. They drove to Jonathon's apartment and Jean didn't go home until Sunday evening.

Jonathon assumed the deal was sealed. It wasn't. On Monday, after both of them got off work, Jonathon called to make sure all was well and to make plans for the evening. When she didn't answer, he was worried. He couldn't have read her wrong; Jean was definitely into him and she was definitely afraid of David. David was possessive, she'd said, and she complained that they often argued. He'd never hurt her, she insisted. He was protective of her and of what he considered his. She didn't answer the second time

Jonathon phoned either and just as he was about to head to her condo, she called him.

"Jonathon," she started, "I adore you." This was good news. "But," (there was that dreaded 'but') we're over. I can't see you again."

At first Jonathon was stunned into silence, paralyzed; then his shoulders relaxed, he began to breathe again, and his brain began to generate language. Before he could speak, though, she went on. "I'm sorry, Jonathon. Goodbye." There was a click that meant disconnection, loss of connection, no more connection. No more conversation. A complete break.

Now, it was mid-July and he sat at the table wondering how long he had been silent. How many women had there been in the chair across from him tonight? Jonathon struggled to refocus on the present moment; was this Lady #3 or #6? Her nametag read Nina. She looked familiar, but he couldn't quite place her. She smiled and he saw it — she looked like Jean. He thought he must be getting a little crazy and was afraid to look up and around the room, afraid that everyone would begin to look to him like some version of Jean.

Jonathon asked, "Do you own a gun, Nina? Do you know how to shoot?"

When he left Jake's, Jonathon tossed away,

one by one, the business cards the women had given him. It wasn't late, just a little after nine. A summer storm had passed through while he was inside. It had apparently rained quite heavily; the air was heavy with humidity. He could see by the lamppost light that the rain on his car, parked across the street, was still dripping. He could hear it dripping off his car, off the buildings, off the trees, dripping in little plunking sounds. It sounded lonely.

Jonathon's desire to shoot seized him on nights like this when the rain made everything quiet and deserted. The Range was just a mile away. He'd bought a 38-caliber special handgun to keep at home, but when he went to the range, he checked out a nine millimeter Glock G43 pistol. The 38 had the mystery of gangster film noir to endear it but the Glock was Gestapo-esque. He liked the feel of it in his hand. He felt ready for anything.

The Range was usually full even on a Tuesday and tonight was no exception. Men and women stood in their stall, legs spread ready for the kick of their selected weapon, each person with live rounds, pointed, at least for now, toward the paper enemy. He'd be lying if he said he didn't think about vanquishing his enemies from time to time, pumping round after round into the immobile body long after his enemy had fallen. It was the mark of a beginner: weapon and enemy rather than gun and target. Video games weren't his thing; pressing buttons on a plastic controller couldn't compare to the experience of holding ammunition in one hand and an open revolver in the other, to the almost erotic pleasure of watching each sleek bullet slide into the cylinder of his 38 or jamming a clip into a Glock. It excited him. But no fantasy was taking place when he aimed and fired at the paper target. The silhouette didn't transform into David Ludlow or anyone else. It was just a paper target. Still, the satisfaction was there, not danger, but the potential for danger inherent in a room full of loaded guns. To know how to shoot with accuracy gave him a confidence that he'd never had.

He bought a shoulder holster for his 38. He decided not to wait an entire month for the speed dating event, strapped on his piece and headed for Jake's Bar and Grill where dames were already milling around waiting for Molly to ring the bell signaling that everyone should take a seat. Certainly, Jonathon's chest was thrust out a little more, certainly he had a more confident smile, and certainly he was more forward with the ladies. It wasn't just his open smile, but he looked at them with refreshed vigor. When lady #1 answered, no, she didn't own a gun, he took her limp hand that rested on the table and said, "Well, you should, Gorgeous. Someone as beautiful as you?" It made her blush and it made Jonathon throw his head back with a hearty laugh. There was a definite swagger to his walk that hadn't been there before, a boldness in his demeanor that was new.

Still, at the end of the evening, he ripped up the cards in plain view of the ladies and threw them in the trash showing his distain that not a single woman had proved to his liking. He vowed to call Jean at work rather than at home the next day, just in case she would be spending her evenings with David. Jonathon needed to make Jean understand that she was in danger from David. After all, hadn't Jean spent three days with him to avoid confronting David on her porch? If that didn't indicate a broken relationship, he didn't know what did.

He didn't go to the shooting range that night but, against his better judgment, drove to Jean's and parked down the street still in sight of her front door and her living room windows. When he didn't have a clear view of her living room, he got out of his car, and walking around back of her place, got up close enough to see into her kitchen window. He couldn't make out what they were saying but he could see through the kitchen door to the living room where David's feet rested on the coffee table. Every once in a while, Jean's hand would come into the frame to pick up the wine glass next to David's feet. Over the weeks that Jonathon had been without Jean, he had become more and more convinced that David had threatened Jean into breaking it off with him. He tried to remain objective, thinking that he had no duty to Jean, but he did, as a male, have a duty to women in general. Maybe Jean wasn't the woman the Universe had brought to him, but he wasn't going to let a woman like her be bullied by a loser like David Ludlow.

Then, Jean's glass was picked up and not put down again. After a few seconds, Jean came walking into the kitchen. At first Jonathon ducked down so as not to be seen but then he saw his opportunity. He raised his head just to where his eyes were above the window sill and pecked with two fingers on the glass.

Her scream was squeaky, no more terrified than if a mouse had run across her foot, but it was enough for David to spring into action. Jonathon ducked again, and knees bent low, ran as fast as he could across her lawn and back toward his car. He fumbled for his car keys, dropped them in the street, retrieved them, hustled into his car and locked the door just as he saw David taking Jean's front steps two at a time. Jonathon's heart pounded as he sped away. David stood in the middle of the street furiously watching Jonathon travel further and further out of his reach.

On his love actuarial table that night, Jonathon gravely added another five micromorts to Jean's score.

At ten o'clock the next morning, Jonathon stepped outside his office and dialed Jean.

"That was a stupid thing you did last night," she said instead of hello. "David's nobody to mess with."

Jean always left him speechless but Jonathon had strapped on his 38 this morning and even in the heat of August wore his suit coat to cover it. "I'm nobody to mess with either, Jean."

On the other end of the phone, Jonathon heard Jean's surprised laugh, a sharp "ha!" as if Jonathon couldn't have been more wrong.

"That's really what I want to talk to you about. I've been studying him and I've determined that the probability of your being hurt or killed by David is fairly high — you have a 60-micromort relationship."

"What? You don't even know him. What are you talking about? Micro what? You're a crazy man. Don't call me again. I'm not answering any calls from you, Jonathon. Not ever. Leave me alone! Do you hear?"

He wanted to tell her that it was a fact that, of all the women murdered in 2015, thirty-three percent of them were murdered by their partners. Conversely, of the men murdered that same year, only three percent were murdered by their wives or girlfriends. She'd hung up, though, before he could warn her.

That night, Jonathon drove by Jean's house again. Over the course of the day, he came to realize that he was the only thing that stood between Jean and abuse or death. He had, without hesitation, appointed himself Jean's personal body guard and he would protect her with his life if he had to. Jonathon parked a little ways away and sat for a minute deciding what to do. He took his 38 out of its holster and checked again to see that it was loaded. Just as he was snapping the gun in its holster again, David rolled down the street. He didn't even get out. Jean, beautiful, long-legged Jean, came bouncing down the stairs and into his car. At first Jonathon started his engine with the intent to follow them, but then he reasoned that they would be having dinner in public and Jean would be in no danger until they were home again. He turned off the engine, opened his window, tilted his seat back, and closed his eyes. A half hour later, he drove through McDonald's and then back to his parking space. An hour and a half later, he went back to McDonald's to buy a cup of coffee and use the bathroom. Another hour passed before he decided to go to a pharmacy and buy a paperback to read, but by the time he got back with the book, it was too dark to read. He moved his car under a street light and retrieved his flashlight from the emergency kit in his trunk. He was on Chapter Fifteen when he fell asleep.

It was past midnight when he woke up. Jean's house was dark. Jonathon didn't see David's car anywhere. He was stiff from sitting. He decided to walk the street to make sure that David's car wasn't there. Jonathon had never been in Jean's house but he could visualize the layout: living room/dining room and kitchen on the first floor, three bedrooms on the second. It was probably the case that the stairs to the second floor were directly in line with the front door and that the door to the master bedroom where Jean surely slept was in line with that or maybe a little to the left of the stairs. He needed to see if she was safe in her bed. If David's car wasn't there, he'd probably gone home, Jonathon reasoned, and Jean would be alone and, chances are, asleep. It wasn't a weekend so she probably hadn't slept over at David's.

Jonathon had stayed around long enough to know that the only security service hired by the community was a vehicle patrol in which the patrolman rarely got out of his car. In his bright, policeman-like uniform, he used the bathroom at the community center and got himself a soda there, but he seldom patrolled the residential area on foot. He was unarmed as far as Jonathon could tell, carrying only a radio transmitter and a stun gun. Jonathon wandered to the back of Jean's unit and looked for points of entry. Her bedroom window was dark, but suddenly, he could see clearly what had happened: while he dozed in the car, David Ludlow had come and gone and Jean was lying strangled and nude in her bed. His vision was clear as day. His purpose had been to save her; he had failed miserably. Yet, perhaps she still breathed. Unable to call for help, Jean lies helplessly hanging on to life. He would have to enter the kitchen window where he had tapped the night before, climb in, and do his best to revive

Jean. The odds were against it, but he had to try.

Jonathon easily entered through the kitchen window and just as easily found the stairs to the second floor in a layout he had rightly anticipated. Instead of bounding up the straight flight, he crept slowly, step by step, with gun drawn. He might have miscalculated and David might still be there somewhere so this precaution was absolutely necessary. It occurred to him that the 38 Special was too small a gun and wished that he had the Glock that he used at The Range. Still, if David was there and unprepared, Jonathon could empty the 38 into him and that should do the job. Even a small bullet placed with precision could be deadly.

The door to Jean's bedroom was half open; Jonathon slid in. It was too dark inside to see more than the outline of Jean's body under the covers. It wasn't the scene he'd imagined of a sprawling, barely breathing nude, but it didn't mean that Jean wasn't in distress.

He went to her bedside and touched her forehead with the back of his hand to see if her body was cold.

Jean jumped and emitted the same squeaky scream she had when she'd seen Jonathon at her kitchen window. Without thinking, she scrambled across the bed and out of the room, grabbing her cell as she passed her night stand. She ran down her stairs and out her door.

"No, Jean, it's me, Jonathon! Don't be afraid. I just came to see if you were okay!"

But Jonathon could hear her giving her location to what he suspected was the 911 operator. He ran down the stairs to show himself, comfort her that it was only him, and that he just wanted to protect her. In his haste, he did not re-holster his 38 but waived it wildly without being aware of what he was doing. He kept yelling, "No, Jean, it's only me, Jonathon. I'm here to protect you!"

He could see that Jean was hysterical and had her eyes riveted on his 38.

"Get away from me! I've called the police. They'll be here any minute!"

Jean looked so beautiful! Her hair all tousled from sleep, her baby blue baby doll pajamas revealing her long, slender legs! Jonathon came down the stairs to where Jean jittered on the sidewalk. Then, she dashed into her house circumventing the stairs and Jonathon could hear the lock crash down. He patiently climbed the stairs back to her front door.

"Jean, I just need to know you're okay. Let me

in, Jean. I'm just here to protect you. Please, let me in." He was very aware that his voice had suddenly gone weak and pleading. He laid his head against the door to make sure he could hear her and tapped the gun on the door, a deadly knocker. "Jean? Are you okay? Please let me in."

Jonathon was so intent on Jean that he heard but ignored the sirens. The police car came barreling up the street, skidded to a stop, and shined its spotlight at Jean's door where Jonathon clung, head still dolefully resting, both hands up next to his ears, one hand clutching his 38.

The officers scrambled out of their car with guns drawn. "Drop the weapon!" they screamed at him in unison. "Drop your weapon!"

"Jean, the police are here. They've got totally the wrong idea and you have to come out and tell them. Jean? Can you hear me?"

If she heard him, she wasn't responding. There was nothing else to do but meet the officers and try to explain. He loved Jean. He wanted to protect her against a violent boyfriend. He was here to save her.

When Jonathon turned, both officers demanded again and again that he drop his weapon, but Jonathon couldn't process it. What was going on? He had to explain. As he approached the officer, clutching his 38, both officers began to fire. As Jonathan Hartwell lay dying on Jean's front porch, he was thinking that he had not calculated his own micromorts. He would have to devise an actuarial sheet for himself when he got home.

Siberia

Martin looks back to smile at me; walking two steps ahead, he takes my hand and leads me as we both follow our taxi driver along the railroad tracks to the train station entrance marked *Intourist*. The morning is gray and everything in sight is shades of the color of the sky save for the dirty, dark green of the trains. It's almost what I'd imagined, this railway station in the small Siberian town of Khabarovsk. Almost. It's more cheerless. Stacks of taped and tied bales are mounded beside the station door. A little girl sits astride one of the bales, a white organza bow the size of a hambone adorns her head. And, the building is more dilapidated than I'd imagined with no hint of any proud past, no badges, emblems or statues, no fading frescos, no flags flying. No commerce is taking place, either. The boarding areas look all but abandoned.

Martin is as relieved as I am that we have come to a place that captures us. We let the driver take our bags and he leads us through a back corridor that looks like a tenement hallway. There's construction rubble half-swept against the wall, a brown apple core, shredded waxed paper, a wooden plank set like a bench that we pick our way around until we reach a room in the midst of renovation. In this room, high, broad windows freshly washed let in light that shines on a clutter of furniture suspiciously like the cheap wood veneer vanity tables and boudoir chairs that languish in storage rooms of second-hand shops across America. Building materials lay in long rows. Ornamental plaster is in piles; the wedding cake ceiling has been taken down in favor of acoustical tile. Our driver leads us past all this to a counter where our tickets will be manually processed, no computers in sight. The only other passenger in the room is a young Japanese man who sits beneath a bright, new sign advertising Mitsui, a Japanese trading company.

Martin and I will be married four years in

December. This is the second marriage for both of us and neither of us have particularly high hopes for this one even though we both ultimately want the same things. It sounds so simple. We want the version of the American Dream that includes a marriage that works, a solid family, children. We take off from harrowing separate work lives to spend time together in some more or less remote spot with some dim hope of improving our chances for making that happen. The first year, it was Bali. The second, Viet Nam. The third year, we went to Tasmania. This year, our fourth, we're taking the Trans-Siberian Railway from Khabarovsk to Lake Baikal.

Through an open door, we can see into the main hall of the station where crowds of people stand in line, baggage in hand. They look like refugees but they are only average Russian rail passengers with ancient suitcases and hobo-like bundles. Whatever reasons there once were for separating foreign passengers from the citizens of the USSR died with the USSR. Nonetheless, we peer at each other from adjacent rooms.

Martin says, "They're curious about us." He looks at me grinning. Martin typically frames his ideas in flat statements. It suggests factual information thus a kind of intellectual superiority, as though he is an astute observer who somehow sizes up a situation with uncanny accuracy.

"I wonder why they keep us separate," I say. I make everything sound like a question. It suggests acknowledgement of Martin's intellectual superiority. I take the low ground, constantly exposing my belly to him.

Martin gives our driver a pack of Marlboro cigarettes as a tip. If he doesn't smoke he can sell the pack for enough rubles for a modest dinner for himself and his wife. Then, I sit down with the luggage while Martin goes to buy two bottles of water and to take a few photographs. Fifteen minutes later, he returns at the end of a group of American tourists who, Vittel tucked tightly under their arms, are being shuttled off to their soft class compartments. They eye us, smile, some wave or speak. Martin and I hang back. Remote is getting harder to find. This gaggle of American tourists, no doubt, took the package tour from Alaska. We'd hoped to avoid them. Some of the men and women wear polo shirts with Bank of America in white letters over the left breast pocket.

My first husband, Marshall, was a banker, I think of these two men as alike as Dalmatians. When Marshall divorced me, I married Martin, a corporate tax attorney. That fact still gives me pause. There's a sense of doom about it, like trading a Malamute for a Siberian Husky.

"Let's go," Martin says, picking up his bags. His voice rings with a mixture of anticipation and dread, confidence and apprehension. There is a courage and enthusiasm in it that both offends and thrills me. I know I would have offered the less commanding, "Shall we go?"

We walk outside along the train platform to hard class car #4, enter the train and find compartment #2. It's next to the matron's compartment and separates us by one from the lavatory. The cabin's floor and fold-down table are littered with egg shells and spots of goo that look like jam. A thin, grimy mattress and pillow are rolled up at the end of the padded leather benches on either side of the cabin. Two more bunks fold down from the wall over the benches. Cotton curtains hang on a string across the grimy window.

Martin is turning in circles in the small cabin. I think he doesn't know what to do or where to put his bags. He doesn't want to set his bag in the stuff we hope is only jam. I stand behind him, then in front of him as he turns, waiting for him to settle. As Martin faces me for the third time, his face brightens. "Sorry," he says over my head, "just give us a minute."

It's the Japanese man from the waiting room. He's left standing in the train corridor, his backpack and gym bag blocking the way to other passengers.

"Under," he says gesturing with his chin. "Space is under." His accent is heavy but we understand him clearly.

Martin lifts the bench frowning and we stow our bags, drop the seat and sit cross-legged to give our roommate access. Martin wets his handkerchief with spit and begins to rub at the goo. The Japanese first checks his ticket against the cabin number and then the berth number, unpacks a few things, stows the rest and then turns to present Martin with his business card, an unreadable squiggle of Japanese characters.

Martin looks at the card, turns it over, hands it to me then extends his hand.

"I'm Martin," he says, shaking hands, "and this is my wife Nealy."

I look up and smile.

"Akio."

Akio is good-looking, tall, and meaty. Young, too. Probably no more than twenty-five.

When the train starts to move, we leave our cabin and stand, fore-arms resting against the sill of the sooty window, watching the train station and Khabarovsk fade from view. It takes only a few minutes to move from town to the countryside. We are going west toward Eastern Europe on a train that will eventually reach Moscow. We pull down the window and let the air rush into our faces. Suddenly, the somber dinginess of the town falls away. Outside the window, trees edge a flat and winding stream. The air is vibrant, the sky tinged with blue and the green expanse of the dense forest is broken only by the vertical white lines of birch trees.

No more than a minute later, down the train corridor, comes a woman practically as wide as the corridor itself. She is dressed in a worn and stained, blue uniform, the blouse of which is too small so gaps between buttons expose both yellowed bra and doughy-white flesh. Her unkempt hair is dyed a coppery reddish-brown and when she smiles at us she shows us four gold teeth. She is the car matron, the absolute authority over her tiny mobile kingdom. Motioning for us to step inside our cabin, we follow her command and sit across from her. Her Russian is peppered with German and a little English. She calls me Fraulein. We understand from her that clean sheets, pillowcases and towels can be gotten for twenty-five rubles each--about fifteen cents. She takes our ticket, placing it in her book destination-side up, takes our fifty rubles and returns in a few minutes with our linens.

We are traveling through the southern edge of Far East Siberia. The river that runs through Khabarovsk serves as a border with China somewhere far out of town. We will come to a place on our trip where we are only miles from Mongolia. At the moment, there is little outside our window but the crystalline lakes of melted snow.

I don't know how readily people take on the characteristics of their environment. It's true that Martin and I were wildly sexual in Bali that first year, acting out the incredibly sensuous landscape, the heat, the passion flowers that dripped from our balcony. We lay on the beach almost naked in each other's arms while everything around us smelled of honey and shone of gold light. That's how first years are. Now, the powerful, vast and unyielding panorama before us distances me from Martin in an unexpected way.

The few towns we pass are clusters of no more than a hundred dwellings, spacious whole log homes built by the grandfather or great-grandfather of the current resident. Often the bright paint of the patterned shutters has weathered to mellow oranges, blues, and greens against the aged brown wood. Vegetable gardens, sprinkled with summer flowers, cover the acre or more immediately adjoin the house. There are no paved roads in the towns and we see no cars parked on lawns or on the dirt roads. We see no heavy farm equipment. In places, there are wooden sidewalks. Except for television antennae and electrical lines, the villages look unchanged for centuries. Even in their primitiveness, the towns have a beauty it would be unfair to label quaint. They're too fierce for such a dainty term. They're more like handsome and terrible old men...men of character and enduring strength. The towns are few and far between and the train doesn't stop at any of them.

But after several hours, we do stop at a town. Ivan, the name we've given to the car matron, stands at the end of the car. We can get off if we want for "sein minuten." Martin and I walk toward a wooden shelter set up about fifteen feet from the train where women who have brought their goods in old baby carriages sell bread, berries, boiled eggs, unsealed bottles of cow-fresh milk and pierogies.

"There were so many gardens, Martin...where're all the fresh vegetables?"

"Unnn," grunts Martin. "Guess they pickle them for winter. These will do."

Martin holds up four fingers to a woman who has brought pierogies to the station in a bucket. She wraps them in newspaper. The sign on her bucket indicates five rubles each.

I would ask Martin what he thinks about the landscape impacting personal relationships but that kind of conversation is too hypothetical for him. He would not be able to speak in declarative sentences. He would sigh a lot and concern himself that I was too abstract. Conversations in which he doesn't make statements and I don't ask questions, the kind in which we both make statements, are, in general, arguments.

"Those women looked like lumberjacks, didn't they, Martin?"

"Yeah, very tough. Survival depends on it. Remember that this is summer when there're fresh vegetables and mild temperatures. Just imagine the winter!"

"So, we're about ten-train-days away from Moscow here, aren't we? Doesn't it strike you that communism really has no meaning here? Or democracy either for that matter?"

"Just to live...whatever it takes to live...that's the politics."

I wonder if communist couples have communist marriages, the political philosophy transferring its values to personal life. From each spouse according to ability, to each spouse according to need. For Martin and me, a capitalist couple, it's more like, what's good for General Motors is good for America. Martin is General Motors; I am America.

The train stops again about nine p.m. Now, we've been glued to the window for about seven hours. We have eaten our pierogi, which turned out to be fried bread dough stuffed with mashed potato. We washed it down with bottled water. A fourth passenger is added to our compartment, a young Russian girl who, it appears, is apologetically forewarned by Ivan that she'll be sharing sleeping quarters with two Americans and a Japanese. She comes in eating the seeds from the center of a freshly picked sunflower.

She appears to be about seventeen years old, blonde, shy and smiling reluctantly. Pretty in a peasant-ish sort of way. She is very thin and wears black jeans and a white blouse.

We introduce ourselves and she nods. Her name is a tangle of unpronounceable Ts and Ws but we each give it a try. She motions for Akio to stand so that she can lift the seat to stow her bag. Then, using the bench for a step, she reaches for a knob over the window and turns on the radio. She reseats herself and picks at the center of the sunflower; it looks as though she is eating the stuffing of a pin cushion.

Siberian summer days do not end until at least ten p.m. Then, the absence of industrial smoke, airplane emissions, or car exhaust allows the night sky to exhibit the glories of a magnificent white moon and millions of stars. It's like a time before the industrial revolution. These scattered villages are populated with fishermen and hunters; they cook and warm themselves with wood burning stoves. They trade fur pelts or wild meat and fish to the woman who bakes bread or makes jam. I smile because I find that strangely romantic.

The radio and lights go off automatically at eleven and all four of us go to bed in our clothes. Under the cover, I pull off my bra through the sleeve of my T-shirt and slip off my jeans. I suspect we all sleep badly, with the train jerking and stopping and the bright moon shining through the window. Still, the clicking of the wheels down the track lull us to sleep eventually. We have been on the train almost twelve hours now and have seen little beyond the exquisite landscape and a few small villages. I know that the train will continue to travel all night through the lush forests that look so rich and past the towns that look so poor.

In the bottom bunk, I hear Martin begin to breathe deeply and evenly. He is a good man and tries to please me but is burdened by the constraint of unfailingly putting himself first. It's something he thinks I should understand. A kind of trickle-down theory.

I am first up in the morning. I tug on my jeans, grab my toilet kit and slip out the door. I'm hoping to get to the bathroom while it is reasonably odor-free from the night's disuse. The stainless steel toilet flushes onto the track and the stainless sink is fed water from an overhead tank. A hole in the middle of the floor allows the car matron to throw a bucket of water across the floor to clean it. It puzzles me that it should smell so bad this early in the trip.

As soon as I leave the toilet compartment, though, I am again mesmerized by the Russian landscape. We have come into a valley floor surrounded by mountains that have a stream winding along their base. The morning mist rises from the land and settles into the mountain gaps.

It's hard to remember when I've seen anything quite as beautiful. I'm uplifted by the pristine quality of the stream that looks clear enough to drink, and by the evergreen covered mountains. It would be nice to stay by the stream for a while but the train moves on.

Martin staggers out of the cabin and makes his way to the lavatory, which is now occupied. He waits, kit in hand, looking mournful like he always does when he has to wait. He loves tedium but only certain kinds. This kind requires patience. He likes the kind that requires diligence. On his way back, he kisses the back of my neck. "Let's go to the dining car," he says.

Are you hungry?" I ask.

Second marriages are always more hesitant than first ones. There's the whole question of love and how our own emotions had betrayed us in our first marriages…we question whether love has any real value. Somewhere along the line, we'd both separated loving behavior from actual love. One never quite trusts. Maybe there is a certain kind of man whom I will always choose, a third marriage to a CPA named Matthew, men as alike as gumballs. And, maybe the kinds of interactions we have with our mates are learned from parents or dictated in genes rather than influenced by larger environments like governments or landscapes.

The trail to the dining car is tenuous. We are, at this point, several cars back from the dining car. The connections between the cars allow us to see the tracks whizzing by beneath us. We cross on a metal strip less than a foot wide, releasing one door only when Martin, who grasps my hand firmly, is securely attached to the handle of the next. Each car varies in its atmosphere. Each car matron's standards leave her mark. One car even smells of air freshener.

When we open the dining car door, every seat is taken by the American tourists. They welcome us mistakenly thinking we are part of their group. The tables are loaded down with brown bread, jam and butter, porridge and coffee. A waitress shoos us out with a wave of her hand. "One hour!" she yells. "Come back one hour!" But I feel exhausted and unwilling. After a bad night's sleep, two arduous trips to the dining car in an hour seems too much.

Outside Ivan's closet-sized room at the end of the car is a hot water tank with a spigot. I'm just about to get some hot water, congratulating myself that I had thought to bring tea-bags, when the matron comes down the corridor toting two glasses of tea that she gives to me and Martin along with sugar cubes wrapped in paper bearing the picture of a train. We are grateful and trot into our cabin to ravage our supply of peanut butter crackers, a parting gift from my sister who dropped us at the airport. I return the cups with a gift of a large chocolate bar and although she seems pleased, I get the impression this was not the reward she is after.

The relentless beauty of the landscape passes our window like a travelogue. By eleven, Akio and Martin are playing chess on a small magnetic board Akio has brought. The Russian girl has sign-language-ed Martin out of his I-pod and is tapping her foot to the music. I alternately stare out the window and read a magazine article about Marilyn Monroe. Then the train stops. Stops in the middle of nowhere. Stops dead center in the middle of nowhere. The Russian girl doesn't seem to notice but just continues to bob her toe to the music.

Then, we hear Ivan booming in and out of each compartment, shaking passengers out of their bunks and off the train. When she storms into ours, Akio picks up his bag but Ivan grabs it and throws it back down onto the seat. "Nyet!" No need to speak twice. She gives him a little nudge on the shoulder and tugs at the foot of the Russian girl to get her moving; then off she rampages to the next cabin.

We are herded off, rushing toward the narrow exit as though the train were on fire. Outside, passengers stand in little clusters not straying far from the tracks. Through the window, I see two uniforms in the first cabin, going through luggage, stripping away bedding, looking in, under and around. One uniform closes the curtains of the cabin she is searching. Our Russian roommate saunters off toward the end of the train still connected to Martin's I-pod. The family from the next compartment sighs and sits down in the grass. The man pulls out a pocket knife and begins to pare his fingernails. From the front of the train, a man in a Bank of America shirt strolls toward us, looking at Martin.

"Any idea what's happening?" he asks Martin. The man has a vise-grip on his calm demeanor. He reeks of the golf course at Hilton Head.

"Looks like they're searching for something." Martin too is determined to be nonchalant. Casually, he shoves his hands deep into his pockets in the same fashion as the man he faces.

The man sucks his teeth and runs the change in his pocket through his fingers.

"Any idea what?"

Martin shakes his head. "Not even an educated guess."

"Ya'all traveling alone?" He glances briefly my way.

Martin nods.

"Going all the way to Moscow?"

"Only as far as Lake Baikal."

"Well..." he says, sucking his teeth again. He shrugs, turns and heads back toward a woman standing in the distance looking anxiously in his direction.

Shared experience seems to separate me from Martin more than ever. I wouldn't have guessed that was possible, but I see him standing there, looking at his watch, then ducking and bobbing his head to see better into the train windows, shifting his weight from one foot to the other and I can almost feel his mind buzzing with the frustration of unanswered questions, with the offense of invaded privacy, with the nauseating effect of having no power. When I think of spending my life with this man, I feel inexplicably bereft. On the other hand, maybe it's just "spending my life" that feels so mournful.

The second year we were married, we were crossing an ochre river in Viet Nam. The ferry was crowded with the kind of men we'd seen everywhere in that country. Cavernous lines gave character to their faces. Rough, callused feet were exposed in plastic sandals. A lean and browned man squatting next to me reached slowly toward my hand and drew it near him to examine. My hand was deadly white in his dark ones. I wore a thin gold ring and bracelet.

In Viet Nam, our lack of calluses qualified us as nobility. We had already stopped being the enemy. We had lost the war but had gotten the best revenge. Martin and I walked the streets like victors, proudly, hand in hand, eating our meals at the Metropole, buying without negotiating. We made love as though we were good at it, better at it than the cyclo-driver who peddled us all the way across Hanoi for a dollar. Still, after two years, we knew no more about our measure of happiness and stability than the day we'd married. Our experience did not translate into knowledge.

Tablecloths are laid out for the American tourists. Bottles of water, bowls of food and plates of brown bread are being set out. We've been waiting an hour. It's lunch. I sit in the grass and pretend to look for four leaf clovers. Martin strides over and tries to re-board the train, the entry of which is guarded by Ivan. I hear him yelling, But our food is in there! Can't I even get something to eat? Ivan stretches her thick arms, barring Martin's way. Oh, for Christ's sake, I hear him mutter as he turns away.

"Do you want to go down to where the other Americans are?" I ask him when he returns. He sits down heavily in the grass beside me. "I'm sure they'd share if you're hungry."

Martin doesn't answer. It's not so much that he wants food as that he wants HIS food. He plants his elbows on his knees and glares into the scrub of the dense forest just beyond the space cleared beside the tracks. It isn't possible to talk now. I'm not in the mood to cajole him. Akio is stretching his legs, trying to speak to other passengers; the Russian girl is nowhere in sight. The sun is warm and I stretch out, lying back in the stiff grass.

After two hours of waiting, we are allowed to re-board the train. The seats have been lifted and our luggage searched, our bags left open. Our linens, mattresses and pillows have been tossed onto the floor. Akio returns with us and emits a sigh of relief to learn that he isn't missing anything. None of us are. Even out stashes of cash are intact. At the far end of our car, Ivan finishes replacing metal panels in the corridor wall.

Martin and I once again stand at the window. Akio follows and stands a little distance away.

"It is common...common?" he considers the word, "usual...ah...usual that European and American couples travel husband and wife, desu ne?"

"Yes," Martin answers.

"Not so usual for Japanese. Husbands travel with...uh...what you call fellow company men. Wives travel with girlfriends." He looks at us questioningly. "Why an American man travel so often with his wife?"

I shrug.

Martin laughs. "I wouldn't want to go on vacation with the guys I work with! I get enough of them at the office."

"I think, Akio," I say leaning past Martin and looking at Akio, "that it's important for a husband and wife to share experience so that later in life they can reminisce together." It embarrasses me to say this in front of Martin. It feels like a lie.

"Reminisce?"

"Recall pleasant times."

"Hai, so desu ne."

"Husbands and wives often enough lead separate lives," I continue instructively. "She's concerned with a career of her own or with cleaning, cooking and raising children and he's concerned with whatever his work is, his office politics, his income. Couples need to share at times when they are both away from their daily concerns. That way, they can devote time to each other."

"Ahhh! Yes, I see. Americans have Christian marriage, yes?"

Martin laughs again, throwing back his head this time. "I would hardly say so, Akio. I was raised a Jew but I'm what you might call a lapsed Jew, if there is such a thing. Non-practicing anyway. Nealy, well, she's a lapsed Protestant is it? Or Catholic?" Martin gives me a questioning look. "Anyway, some lapsed thing or another. Christian marriage? I don't think so!"

"Well," Akio says, "I would like someday to be a couple like you!" He looks at his shoes for a minute and then goes on, "In Japan, we have famous writer…Mishima. You know?"

I look at Akio blankly but Martin says, "He's that guy that committed ritual suicide, isn't he? In the sixties maybe?"

Akio looks at Martin as though he's struggling with his facial expression. Perhaps, he finds that Westerners know only this about Mishima. "Mishima wrote many famous works. He says a man and a woman need a third thing to, uh," he lowers his head and mutters in Japanese trying to find the words, "make work the marriage. For him, the third thing is the Emperor of Japan. Maybe for you, Martin and Nealy, third thing is Siberia."

Akio stands two windows down seemingly absolutely aching at the beauty of the landscape and I wonder if there is such a thing as too beautiful, too peaceful. In an odd way, we have been humbled and cleansed by the acts of the uniformed invaders. Some tension that we hadn't even known was there has been relieved or perhaps redirected. We had been violated, cleared of suspicion and found to be innocent of some treachery we couldn't even conceive.

Even though it's fairly late afternoon, we decide to journey to the dining car once more. The American tourists having been fed, we may have a chance at getting served. We sit down at a booth and wait. A woman standing at the front of the car is filling the napkin holders, first cutting the napkins in half. We eat a salad of diced cucumbers and boiled potatoes with an oil dressing and fried bread and jam, a lunch that reminds me of *The Grapes of Wrath*. I'm thinking of Rose'a'shar'n mixing flour and water and frying it in bacon fat.

Martin orders tea and I decide to risk coffee. I am brought a demitasse of murky liquid not quite coffee-color. The taste is not bad, though, once I strain the grounds through my teeth. As we sit there, the train once again comes to a station and stops. There is the same gathering as at other stations, the women under a wooden shelter with their goods, women with buckets of pierogi or boiled potatoes sold in newspaper cones. The train's cook signals a farmer who carries a bucket of berries. The cook dumps them into a cardboard box and returns the bucket to the farmer. I imagine berry pies, pancakes, and muffins and wonder what the tattooed and T-shirted cook plans to do with so many berries.

No bill is offered to us and when Martin asks how much we owe, the waiter hesitates a moment and then asks for three American dollars. It is more than we've paid for larger meals in Russia but less than we'd paid for espresso in New York. There is no doubt that the American dollars go into the Russian waiter's pocket without a moment's thought of government employers.

Our car matron has been on the look-out for our return and when she sees us, she approaches us excitedly. Chattering away, she takes Martin's arm and turns him toward the train window inside our compartment. What had been a milky profusion of dirty clouds now sparkles with bright clarity.

"Reward!" she beams. In half English-German-Russian, half charades, we understand that she is given "extra points" by the uniforms for the presence of American tourists but that the presence of the Japanese had earned her nothing. The clean window is her treat for us. She cocks her head and motions for us to follow her into her small office. The room is no more than a closet with dials and controls covering one wall. The three of us in the room almost touch noses. She has an array of silver glass holders, the kind we'd used this morning. She wants five American dollars for each for them. They have Sputnik embossed on all but one and that one has a Napoleon-esque male figure atop a horse. I decide on two of them and Martin hands her ten dollars. Enthused by our response, she next shows us a bottle of vodka. "Putin" she says pretending to down a shot, "Medvedev" she says making the motion again. She writes seventeen American dollars on a scrap of paper. She explains, motioning with her hands and scribbling down $300, that she wants to go to America and she needs only three hundred more American dollars.

We act pleased that she is interested in coming to America but decline her offer to sell us Vodka.

After a little more than thirty hours on the train, our cabin is littered with berries, cracker crumbs and a half bottle of water. In the bottom of the clear green glass of the bottle, which sits in the sun of the window, brown fuzz floats. Our Russian roommate has returned with no sign of Martin's I-pod. When he tries to question her, she pretends to understand nothing. The matron is yelling at someone for opening the window during the part of the day that the air conditioning is on. I peek out our open cabin door at her. The man protests, but the matron wins out in the end and the window is closed.

At a long stop at a station, we opt to buy nothing, choosing instead to eat our California raisins and nuts. The end of our trip is near and we decide to take the risk that the Intourist food will be better.

Sometimes the Russian girl locks us all out of our cabin. We think only that she is changing clothes or craving a moment alone. Once though, as we are all lolling about reading, she stealthily removes our binoculars from her bag and places them on the floor then scoots them a few inches in our direction. It is unlikely that Martin will see his

I-pod again without a fight. We sit amid our bag of food, binoculars, cameras, books, magazines, and clothes that spill obscenely across our side of the car while the Russian girl sits eating her boiled egg and sunflower seeds. Later, she walks down the corridor and strikes up a conversation with an Asian-looking girl with bleached hair and a definite black-eye.

There are children in the car who steal glances at us and one little boy who flirts outrageously with us and jabbers at us not in the least puzzled that we respond with words he can't understand. He smiles and we give him a small chocolate bar. Shortly, he returns with a peach for us.

The day passes. I stretch out on the bottom bunk for a short nap while Martin stands at the window. When I wake up, I am alone in the car. Martin, the Russian girl, and Akio have all gone off somewhere. I'm longing for a cold drink but even the dining car has nothing refrigerated or iced. I go out into the empty corridor. Through open cabin doors, I see families napping or staring silently out the window. I open the window a bit and lean into the refreshing air. Then, I hear the lock of the toilet compartment click and see Martin standing in the corridor, his hand still resting on the compartment door handle. He seems surprised to find me in the corridor.

"Nealy, you're awake. Come with me. I need something to drink." He jerks his head to emphasize his request that I accompany him. He opens the train car door and steps out onto the narrow bridge between the cars and holds out a hand to me.

After I pass the lavatory that Martin has just left, the door opens again and I glimpse the Russian girl on her way out. She is looking down, checking her clothes, then she looks up. Seeing me, she steps back in and closes the door again.

Martin says nothing. Only reaches for my hand. "Come on," he says, "I'm thirsty."

"What's going on, Martin?" I ask but he doesn't answer. The noise of the train is loud outside the car; still, I believe he heard me. I feel emotionally flooded and it stops me. In the dining car, I shut down completely as we drink our warm cola. This is like me. I can't speak. I want proof and yet the proof is right in front of me.

Later, all four of us are lying around the cabin. The train is moving very slowly and so is time. Martin's head rests on my lap. It feels like his way of holding me down. I can think of nothing but the Russian girl looking down to check her clothes. It's obvious they were in the lavatory together.

Martin's head is vulnerable in my lap.

Through our now clean window, I see farmers cutting hay, using scythes and piling the hay on long poles to be dragged away. They work in groups; some look like family groups, and when the hay is in ricks, they sit under a tree together and rest. Sometimes a cloth is spread and covered with bottles and loaves of bread. We see a truck hauling the hay less often than we see a horse and wagon. Only once in a thousand miles have we seen a tractor. The image of three Russian men rhythmically swinging their scythes remains with me when I close my eyes.

When we reach Ulan Ude, the Buryat capital, Akio and Martin are asleep, books open on their chests. The Russian girl is plugged into Martin's I-pod once again. Across the back of the I-pod, in red nail polish, she has written something I would guess is her name. The train car seems smaller than before...more confining...stifling.

I gaze out the window in our cabin continually overwhelmed by the vastness of this somber country. Summer in Siberia lacks the frivolity of summer in California. In Siberia, summer is hustle, a fevered opportunity to harvest, a respite from the bitterness of winter. It is not the idleness of a lazy afternoon spent by the pool. Surviving the winter means capitalizing on summer.

From the direction of our door, Ivan is hissing and motioning me to step outside. She takes my arm as I struggle to disentangle myself from Martin.

"Baikal", she says smiling. I gasp...literally, gasp. Before me is an expanse of water surprising even in this country of overwhelming vistas. It is the largest fresh water lake in the world, some four hundred miles long, forty miles across and a mile deep. It looks like a sea. I rouse Martin and Akio.

The lake comes in and out of view, the railroad tracks at times almost on the shore of the lake and then falling back behind trees. We stand awed, waiting for the next glimpse. I look at Akio whose eyes are glossy, near tears. Since he was ten years old, it had been his dream to ride this train. "When I see the lake," he says, "I am so impressed, I can not express my feeling."

We pass a group of people swimming who wave to the passing train. Some boys playing on a rock on the shore make us laugh when they moon us. We are still perhaps two hours from the end of our journey. The car matron makes one last capitalist advance, offering us a white shawl for twenty dollars. When we decline, she brings us tea and pins wings on our T-shirts. The wings are emblems that we've been passengers on the Trans-Siberian Railway, she tells us. When I return the empty cups, I give her five American dollars. She smiles--this is the reward she's been waiting for.

The train again stops for no apparent reason and again we wait for it to start up. There are only a few small fishing boats on the lake. No resort hotels dot the shores. The water is so clear that we can see the bottom of the lake near the shore from the train window.

"This lake contains more water than all the Great Lake's put together and it even has its own fish. It's called an Omul and it's not found anywhere else in the world." I had read the same *National Geographic* article as Martin but I'm not ready to stop him from espousing his declarative sentences. "Over three hundred streams feed into Lake Baikal and only one runs out. And, picture this: in winter, the entire lake is frozen! Almost a century ago, railroad tracks were laid across the frozen lake for supplies to be brought in. A supply train on a frozen lake! Imagine it!" We are both silent then, our attention riveted on the scene out the train window.

Then I say, not expecting to, "Martin, what

were you doing in the bathroom with that Russian girl?" If I had thought, I would have transformed the question into a declarative sentence.

Martin frowns. "What a bizarre thing to ask, Nealy!"

"She was in there with you, Martin, I saw her. You traded your I-pod for a blow job or for a quick fuck, didn't you?"

"You have a wild imagination," he says and turns back to the view out the window of the slowly moving train. "Don't spoil this moment, Nealy."

"Martin, it wouldn't be the first time." I keep my eyes on him. I'm angry but my words come out as though I'm only curious or at most disappointed.

He is agitated, of course, not because he'd been caught, but because I am being more confrontational than he's used to. He has successfully talked me out of believing my own eyes before and he's setting out to do it again.

"I know what I saw, Martin," I say.

There is a tremendous loneliness about the silent landscape, and a kind of terror too, as though the winter could suddenly replace the summer, freezing everything to stone and covering the train with snow until even it disappeared.

Martin is struggling to neutralize his agitation and to recapture his awe. The tracks have drifted away from the lake and he looks hard through the trees to see if he can still catch some sliver of it.

Did I say Martin is very good looking? That he dresses well? That when I moved into his house, it was more tastefully decorated than my own? Did I say that Martin switched us to online bill pay before I ever even learned to access the Facebook he'd set up for me? Did I say that Martin's mother, father and older brother are exactly like him?

Last year, Martin and I went to Tasmania. In Port Arthur, we toured the ruins of the penal colony. The tangerine light swept across the bay into the vacant windows of the mill where the prisoners had ground their grain. We were staying nearby in a bed and breakfast transformed from prison settlement housing. We had rented a car and were alarmed at the number of carcasses of wallaby road kill that littered the highway between the penal colony and the settlement house. Martin drove slowly the three miles between the two places. In Tasmania, we were primitives, I suppose, our relationship simplified into dodging wombats and wallabies, our lovemaking unsophisticated.

Martin has gone back into the cabin while I remain ready to take in the next glimpse of Lake Baikal. Most passengers have left their cabins to huddle in the corridor and, like me, look out the window. A few, those not going on to Moscow, already have their luggage ready at their feet. Martin raises the seat and begins to gather our belongings. He takes my bag from storage and sets it on the floor. He stuffs my magazine into the side pocket. Martin glances at the Russian girl who ignores him, her eyes cast down on her hands clutching the I-pod, her feet tapping along to the music.

The town of Irkutsk is beginning to show signs of its existence. Log houses are giving way to apartment blocks. Paved roads are beginning to appear. Cars and busses become more frequent. The train is moving very slowly now; it is a matter of minutes before we arrive at the train station.

"We're almost there," Martin tells me. "She doesn't have much," he volunteers pulling our bags into the corridor. "Let her have the I-pod. I'll get another one."

Perhaps relationships are impacted by how commerce is carried out, what the goods are, how things are bartered. There is a simultaneous poverty and richness about Siberia that has to do with the richness of the land and it's stubbornness in yielding that richness to the people who live there, in yielding it to the young Russian girl. There is no generosity about Siberia, no gentleness, only a demand that life be lived harshly amidst the gift of the landscape's splendor.

    At the station, Martin wrestles our bags off the train and moves them out of the way of the other passengers. He looks small standing there surrounded by our immodest luggage. Still, with the low covering over the platform, the station squarely behind it and Irkutsk barely in the distance, we are moving into a landscape of more human dimension.

Jo Rousseau

The Island in Winter

After two tries, the fire finally catches. Ellen shoves in the last two sticks of wood, but the cottage is still chilly; the little stove sucks up the wood faster than the small room can be warmed. She stands, disapprovingly, watching the wood disappear as if it were tissue paper. The woodshed is practically outside her door but, unreasonably, she dreads going there. Woodsheds are places where straps are taken to misbehaving boys, she thinks, and where young girls lose their innocence. But not this woodshed; it's an open canopy where no possibility exists for boys to be taught a lesson nor for young girls to be seduced. Still, she stands with her hands on her hips, looking down at the stove as if it were a naughty child.

It's early morning and when the fire dies again, Ellen decides to leave the stove cold. It's been almost fifteen years since she last stayed on Whidbey Island; her immunity to the damp chill of the island has been lost. There is familiarity, though, in the winter mornings that never seem to blossom into day but slink from sunrise to sunset on a shallow arc of the horizon. She sits at the kitchen table looking out at the morning brightening to gray light over Useless Bay.

When the sun is an hour higher in the sky, Ellen sees Munroe standing in front of his house just down the dirt road from her cottage. He's looking at his truck. He is the caretaker of the cottages, seven cottages in all, six of them empty now with Ellen as the only winter guest. Munroe does hard physical labor all day long, swinging axes, painting trim on the cottages, repairing rooftops, but when Ellen looks him in the eye, he seems dreamy, laidback. Perhaps his body reflects the reality while his eyes reflect his desire. Munroe wears lanky jeans and plaid flannel shirts, work boots most of the time, but this morning he sports cowboy boots. A cowboy hat sits on his head almost resting on his ears. Munroe is heartbreakingly handsome with perfect, rugged flaws in his skin and perfectly unruly hair always trying to escape a secure hat. Munroe promised to take Ellen into town to rent a car. She wants to prepare for Alistair who will be coming in on the three o'clock ferry.

Lisa comes out of their house, and Munroe and Lisa stand by his truck, seemingly in quiet disagreement. Lisa's hand engulfs her ever-present coffee cup, her elbow digs into her waist, her arm rising as though she is about to take a sip and yet she never seems to. Lisa is a pretty woman even if she's a little plain. Her hair is blond and thin. It has a bit of perm to give it some body. Her skin is tired with caring for her twins; her housedress, a shirt-waist, has faded blue flowers giving her the look of a woman enduring the hardships of the dust-bowl depression. Every few minutes Lisa looks back over her shoulder, through the screen door, and into the house where the twins play.

Ellen decides to walk down to the farmhouse rather than wait for Munroe to drive up. As soon as she leaves her cottage, Lisa glances Ellen's way, then heads into the house.

Munroe smiles, waves, climbs into his truck. Ellen quickens her step, jumps in the passenger seat. Inside, Munroe's truck smells of wet dogs and llama feed. His dash is covered with maps and receipts and crumpled up cigarette packs. Waxed paper still has the remains of a sandwich—the unwanted bread crust. There are at least three open packs of spearmint gum. Munroe's hands are clean, even his nails, and he's newly shaven and combed. He's even put on some aftershave or maybe it's cologne. He is still in his work clothes, though. He asks Ellen to buckle up, which she does. Then, he throws the truck in reverse, lays his arm across the seat to look back over his shoulder, and speeds down the dirt driveway, making a sweeping arc at the end of it onto the paved road.

It's November and when Munroe drops Ellen off at Island Car Rental, the office windows are dark and the building looks empty. Half-way out of the truck she turns and says, "You sure there's someone here?"

"Yep. Oh, he may be next door at the café drinking coffee but he'll see you. And if he don't, go over to the café and tell Ted you need a car."

The first time Ellen saw Munroe, she'd imagined his voice low, deep to match his cowboy persona, but Munroe's voice is high and chirpy. She almost laughs every time he speaks. Maybe that's why he doesn't say much.

The car rental office is a mobile unit at the back of a half-full parking lot. She tries the door. It's unlocked but the place is empty, so she walks the few yards to the café and spots what is surely Ted sitting at the counter chatting up the waitress.

It's a kind of old-fashioned, gingham-curtained café. Homey. Friendly. Ted sits at the counter; the only other customer is a man sitting in a booth next to the window reading a newspaper spread fully open, his arms stretched beyond his coffee and fried eggs to turn the crackly pages. Everyone looks up when Ellen shuts the door behind her.

"You must be Ted," she smiles and walks toward him.

He slides off the stool and extends his meaty hand, "You got that right. What can I do you for? You looking to rent a car?"

Soon Ellen is settled into a metallic blue Ford Focus. She follows the main street of the town to find the grocer where she buys a couple of steaks, a box of instant rice pilaf, and some vegetables for a salad. She buys ground coffee regretting that she'd forgotten to check for a coffee maker; she can't remember what Alistair takes in his coffee so buys milk and sugar just in case. She checks the shelves for wine, but finding the selection poor, decides to visit the winery before she picks up Alistair at three.

Alistair. It had been a stolen weekend all those years ago when she was here with him. It was exactly this time of year, just before Thanksgiving, fifteen years ago? Yes, fifteen years, but maybe more. They worked at the same company in those days, gotten tangled up with each other over the copy machine when he'd caught her stealthily copying her divorce papers. Alistair was kind, sympathetic, and she was needy then, vulnerable, an emotional wreck. Later that day, he asked her if she wanted to get a drink after work. They could talk, he said.

She never once thought of herself as the *other woman*. She had been needy, yes, but at least she was in recovery; need, she found out, was Alistair's perpetual condition. For some, neediness is programmed into their being. Ellen and Alistair depended on each other for years until Ellen needed more than just a lover. She needed more and she wanted that more to come from Alistair.

"I didn't sign up for that," he admonished her, his forehead wrinkling into a red V between his eyes. "I love my wife and I wouldn't leave my children. This isn't a surprise, Ellen. You knew this from the beginning. I haven't tricked you."

Ellen vowed to move on, but Alistair was unavoidable at work. He would run into her at the copier and their hands would touch and, before they knew it, lunch was at the nearest motel. Then, they began to fight over meaningless things as unsure lovers do. She paid for the room because Alistair couldn't take the chance his wife would see it on his credit card. He'd promise to repay her but there was always an excuse: no cash, new soccer shoes for Justin, some payment due. How could she not feel used? But they didn't stop. Expectations dwindled until all that was expected was the willingness to offer up a naked body. It must have been enough then.

It was bound to happen, though. Sooner or later, Alistair was offered a promotion. The company was branching out and needed someone to head up an office in Denver.

"Seattle will always be the main office." Alistair said as though she was the one who needed to be comforted, "I'll be back for meetings all the time." It was evening; Monica had left that morning with the kids to house hunt in Denver, happy that the move took her closer to her sister in Boulder. Alistair had stayed behind because his workload had gotten ridiculous now that he was vacating his old job, training the new man, tying up loose ends.

Ellen thinks all of this as she puts her few groceries away in the cabinets of Cabin #1, Owl Cottage, so called because of the owls that hooted perpetually from a nearby roost. There is Moon View Cottage, and Waterfall Cottage, each one named after some local specimen of natural beauty.

Ellen vowed again and again to move on but somehow she never did. Something about Alistair bound them together, something she couldn't identify, or so went the typical thinking of Ellen…that her attachment to Alistair was something supernatural, something out of her control…some magic in him and not some flaw in her. It's a serious error.

Finding no coffee pot in the cabin, Ellen wonders if one of the other cottages has one that she might use. She should ask Lisa. Besides, she wants to ask her about the winery, how to get there and whether it's worthwhile.

It's just after noon, less than three hours until Alistair. Ellen wanders down to the farmhouse to find Lisa playing on the living room floor with the twins, Emmy and Grace. Ellen knocks and Lisa calls for her to come in. The kitchen is warm and smells of fresh coffee but the brightness of the yellow wallpaper faded long ago. The wooden countertop shows a circle of dark wood where the cistern pump was removed to make way for indoor plumbing. Spots of worn linoleum look like footprints that Lisa has put a shining finish on, immaculate except for the Cheerios making oat-y polka dots around the kitchen table legs.

Ellen doesn't plan to spend any time with Lisa but seeing her there in the company of her infants draws Ellen into the living room where she sits down in a frazzled easy chair. This room has the same half-remodeled quality as the kitchen: brown wallpaper with tiny blue and yellow flowers, a bare spot at the corner of the ceiling where a leak had been patched, beige linoleum floor worn through in spots. The furniture huddles in the center of the room, a long couch with a blanket spread in front of it where the children's toys are scattered, easy chairs with side tables, a big iron stove with a fire screen in front of it to protect the children.

"I don't want to keep you…" Ellen starts but Lisa interrupts immediately with her laughter

"My God, Ellen, I pray for someone to 'keep' me! I love my girls but they aren't exactly brilliant conversationalists and I have a feeling it's going to be quite a while before they are. I'm glad you came! Let me get you a cup of coffee."

"No, no, really, Lisa, I can only stay a minute. I'm picking up my friend in a few hours, and I have some errands to tend to. I just dropped in to ask about a coffee pot for the cottage and whether the winery is worth a visit."

Ellen doesn't really have errands, but passing the time with Lisa will not allow Ellen to muse about Alistair. Thinking of Alistair, only of Alistair, requires solitude, a kind of wrapping herself in the world of Alistair to the exclusion of almost everything else. She wants to savor this time anticipating his arrival, and she wants nothing more than to dwell on the moment he steps off the ferry to be met by her eager arms. She imagines herself happy for the first time in a long time.

Ellen is in the habit of counting her chickens before they hatch. It's why her credit cards are maxed out, always counting on money that's not yet in her pocket. She counts on promotions before they're offered, counts on happy-endings before the movie is half-finished. She is fatally optimistic.

Ellen takes a kind of perverse pride in Alistair. Lisa, Ellen thinks, is surely curious about someone referred to as "my friend," but Lisa doesn't ask. Ellen considers offering up the titillating information, but decides against it. Lisa will see Ellen drive up to the cottage with Alistair in the passenger seat, see them go into the cottage together, his suitcase in his hand. It's only a short time now. Ellen wants to go. Lisa, though, is compelling with her washed out look. Here is Lisa on an island in winter, empty cottages all around her, and a husband who shines up to go to town. So, Ellen takes Lisa up on coffee after all and settles into the frazzled chair and they talk. Not long after that, the girls are asleep on the blanket and Lisa is pushing back her hair in a gesture of relief.

Lisa's eyes suggest that she has an old soul, as if she knows things other people don't know, things like how insignificant the Earth is in the Solar System and how it is even more insignificant in the Universe. It's a knowing that stays in Lisa's awareness and informs her decisions. She knows how insignificant wars are, how meaningless, with their death tolls, with their bloodshed, and how insignificant human suffering is and that every human suffers because it is the fate of all humans to suffer. She knows that, in the scheme of things, nothing really matters, no, not at all, not in the long run. Human history is irrelevant; the stories of billions of people go undocumented, not just forgotten, but obliterated except for some that are feebly written on yellowed documents, a family tree, forgotten in a cedar chest in the attic. Worst of all, Lisa already knows that Munroe will leave her, maybe not today, maybe not for years, but he will leave; she knows she can't keep him.

Ellen looks at Lisa and sees how tired she is. There is something comforting about Lisa, though, an acceptance maybe, a determination not to struggle against life but to embrace whatever comes. It's a kind of surrender, not to the enemy but to love.

Lisa feels part of something bigger, part of the infinite history of the entire Universe. Munroe has not made her feel insignificant; she *IS* insignificant as are Ellen and Monroe and Ellen's friend. But, for Lisa, what is not insignificant are Emmy and Grace. They are the world; they are the Universe.

The sound of Munroe's axe is a steady and rhythmic thwack, thwack, thwack. Lisa seems spent now that the girls are sleeping, so Ellen sets down her coffee cup and gets up to go just as the thwacking stops.

Ellen passes Munroe on the path between her cottage and the farmhouse. Munroe doesn't look up, doesn't greet her, simply walks past her with his head down, whistling gently through rough lips. His axe swings loosely from his hand.

Munroe takes off his muddy work boots and hangs his hat on the hook just inside the door. Lisa is asleep on the couch, the girls asleep on the blanket on the floor in front of her. Seeing them anchors him, makes him feel, no, not proud, but relieved in some way, as though he's fulfilled his mission as a man, the purpose for his existence. Oddly, this feeling, though unformulated in Munroe's mind, does not warm him. In fact, his sense is that the completion of his task in the chain of human existence creates a distance from them. He's done what he's had to do and now his life is his own.

Munroe unbuttons his shirt and gets ready for his shower.

Lisa doesn't hear Munroe come in but when Grace begins to gurgle, Lisa is suddenly awake. She hears the shower then; she sees Munroe's boots and hat by the door. Emmy is still sleeping peacefully, but Grace, into a pre-crawl scooting phase, is on the move. This is important and Lisa follows Grace without stopping her or helping her, just watches Grace's progress across the floor until she reaches the easy chair and reaches up to try to pull herself up into a standing position. Emmy squirms, beginning to awaken. Lisa picks up Grace, secures her in her high chair, and puts a handful of Cheerios on her tray, then heads back for Emmy.

Earlier in the day, Lisa put a pot roast in the oven and now the aroma of it fills the house. She takes two plates from the cabinet and sets them on the table. Munroe will be hungry when he finishes in the shower. But when Munroe appears at the kitchen door, he's dressed to go out, not to sit down to dinner.

"You aren't going out so soon, are you, Munroe?" Lisa is disappointed. She's beyond disappointed — she's scared. "You're going to have dinner first, right?"

"I have to get Albert over to Mystic Farms." Albert is the stud llama. "Then, I promised the boys I'd stop by for a drink or two." He says this without looking at her. He's heading for his hat. "Smells good though." Munroe comes back to the table to pick up one of the biscuits from the bowl that Lisa has just set down. He munches into it giving Lisa a quick wink and spits crumbs as he tells her that he'll be back early.

He won't be back early, Lisa already knows, and the boys aren't waiting on him. He doesn't put on cologne for the boys.

It isn't that Lisa fails to be furious, but that she

contains her fury. After all, in the big picture, it means very little. She hears Munroe's truck start up and then the headlights move down the driveway and disappear onto the road. She moves the bowl of biscuits back to the stovetop and prepares to feed the twins. She thinks about calling Ellen to ask if she wants to come down for dinner, but remembers that her friend has probably arrived by now and sees that Ellen's car isn't in front of the cottage. Lisa thinks of Munroe pushing the radio buttons on his truck.

Munroe presses number four, the country music station. There's never any traffic in winter, at least not until the commuter ferry when everyone is coming home from work. He thinks of driving home afterward and how he loves the way his headlights show a short distance in front of him. He loves the way so few houses will have their lights on by the time he drives back. He will hum down the road the happiest man on Whidbey Island. Munroe stops to load Albert into the open flatbed of this truck, tying a tether to each side. He chuckles, turns up the volume on the radio a bit, and thinks that he will deliver two studs to Mystic Farms, one for Cheri's llama and one for Cheri.

Earlier, around two-thirty, Ellen looked for a spot in a practically full lot. The commuter run isn't until five; then, the lot will empty out. Finding a spot just when she was about to give up, she goes to stand where the walk-on passengers debark.

Munroe drives down the road headed to Cheri and to Mystic Farms while Lisa plays on the floor with the twins. Ellen stands waiting at the dock.

A very light mist is falling; Ellen pulls her parka hood up and ties the cord under her chin; a thick layer of dark clouds still can not hide a ray of light from the fading sun. Ellen can't yet see the ferry coming, but there are already a few people waiting. The island isn't that popular in the winter, still couples come to stay at the bed and breakfasts for a weekend, paddle canoes, ride bikes, walk the beach.

Now, Alistair's kids have gone off to college and his wife has gone with her sister to Paris. He has two weeks. He knew Ellen would travel to Whidbey, to the island where they had shared Owl Cottage. He called.

Someone said that insanity is continuing to do the same thing over and over while expecting different results. When Ellen picked up the phone and heard Alistair's voice, it was like a corner had been turned. Yes, she would meet him. Yes, she would rent "our" cabin. Yes, she would pick him up at the ferry. Yes, yes, yes. This time, things would be different.

In Ellen's mind, Alistair looks exactly the same as he did fifteen years ago. Neither gained nor lost an ounce, every hair on his head still there.

She can see the ferry now.

She is sure she'll have no trouble recognizing him but, as the ferry draws nearer, she re-imagines him as a balding man with glasses, a jacket hanging loose to cover a paunch. And, what about her? She is maybe ten pounds heavier — okay, maybe twenty. The long hair she had the last time they met is cut short. She's been careful about wrinkles around her eyes and mouth, but nothing stops the march of time completely.

Alistair chose to age with his wife, to grow old with her, to accept the changes in her face and body in rhythm with his own, and ultimately to be buried next to her. Fifteen years! Ellen has known other men, of course, but she knows with certainty that if the head on the pillow next to hers isn't Alistair's then it is the wrong head, with the wrong face. Everyone else is simply the wrong man. Anyone else is just anyone else. Those men were like tourists passing through her bed until Alistair would make up his mind to find his way back to her.

Oh, Ellen!

The ferryboat horn blasts. The men are already in place to moor the boat. Those waiting begin to stir. Two children next to Ellen jump up and down excitedly, smiling up at their mother who watches the ferry approach. The walk-ons begin to flow down the plank and Ellen straightens her jacket, removes her hood. She stretches herself, standing on her toes, craning her neck, searching for his familiar face no matter the changes. Couples wheeling their bikes beside them, a group of boys with camping gear and a canoe, men and women in suits, men in work clothes, carpenters, repairmen, a woman and her dog all walk down the ramp to the dock. Maybe Alistair decided at the last minute to use the bathroom, or maybe he didn't realize how close they were to docking. Maybe he was just ordering up a coffee when the horn sounded.

But then, all the cars are off, all the passengers off, and the signal is given to load the embarking cars and passengers.

A thousand things could have happened. A delayed flight, a missed ferry. There is no cell phone service at the cottage, but there is at the ferry terminal. Ellen takes out her phone and calls Alistair, his number still on her speed dial.

Alistair doesn't answer. Ellen sits in a coffee shop, waiting to see if he will arrive on the five o'clock commuter run. When the five o'clock comes, Ellen waits with the same anticipation as she did for the three o'clock. But he doesn't come. Ellen doesn't tell herself that Alistair isn't coming. She tells herself that he is delayed. She doesn't say that he isn't answering his phone. She tells herself that he must be in an area with no service. Ellen doesn't want to go back to the cabin without him. There is another ferry at eight and then a final one at ten. He is not a thoughtless man. Something must have happened.

Ellen returns to the coffee shop to wait for Alistair's call and the eight o'clock ferry. But Alistair doesn't call and her calls to him go unanswered. She's worried. She's sure he is on his way but something frustrating or even terrible must have happened. When he isn't on the ten o'clock, Ellen pulls her jacket up around her neck and heads for her car.

The grocer is still open. He closes at eleven and, after waiting until the last man had left the ferry, she barely makes it to buy herself a bottle of much needed wine — well, actually, she buys two.

When she passes the farmhouse, Munroe's truck isn't there and the kitchen light is on. Lisa sits at the kitchen table thumbing through a magazine. Ellen hesitates long enough for Lisa to spot her and get up from her chair to go to the window where she waves Ellen in.

Lisa holds the door open and Ellen dashes in. It has gotten cold. The drizzle stopped long ago, but there is a chill wind, damp with the rain yet to come.

"Coffee?" Lisa offers.

Ellen pulls the bottle of wine from its bag. "Wine?"

Lisa smiles, puts the mugs back and gets down two juice glasses.

"You have a corkscrew?" Ellen asks.

Lisa rummages through a drawer and pulls out a fancy one that Ellen turns over in her hands before figuring out.

They sit down at the table but neither woman starts the conversation. They are tired, worn out from a long day, and from the stresses the day has brought them. Then Lisa says as if it has just occurred to her, "Your friend? Didn't she come?"

Ellen shakes her head. "Maybe tomorrow." But Ellen can't even imagine sitting in the coffee shop all day waiting for the ferries one after the other and watching them empty out until she's the only one standing there.

"What happened?" Lisa wants to know.

Ellen shrugs. "Apparently something that prevents him from calling."

Lisa understands with the masculine pronoun something, something in the vast universe of the unknowable, something about women and the men they wait for and she wonders how she and Ellen are ever going to stop waiting.

"What are you looking at?" Ellen points to the magazine.

"Christmas cookie recipes." Lisa turns the magazine toward Ellen. "You have kids?"

"I wasn't that lucky. I was married once for a short time and I always thought that someday I'd marry again. Someday I'd find the right man and have some kids, but…" Her voice is trapped behind pursed lips.

"I don't know what I'd do without my girls." Lisa has immediate regrets. What kind of thing is that to say to a childless woman? "But, I imagine you have a freedom that I can't even imagine." She tries to recover.

Ellen shrugs. "Certain kinds of freedom aren't worth having. Not all freedoms are created equal."

It's past midnight when Ellen goes to her car for the second bottle and after two by the time she makes the short drive to her cottage. Gratefully, she falls into bed and is asleep before her head hits the pillow.

Through the cottage window and down the dirt path from Ellen, Lisa waits for Munroe to come home. Ellen downed the better part of the two bottles while Lisa kept herself alert. Grace wakes and after some soothing goes back to sleep, but Emmy wakes as soon as Grace is back in her crib. Lisa lies beside Emmy on the blanket on the floor, stroking her back until her baby is asleep again. But Lisa can't sleep; she watches television, the paid programming that's on late night, then turns it off and sits in the dark and quiet of her living room. After a while, she stretches out on the couch and falls into a light sleep.

Up the way in the rental cottage, Ellen sleeps restlessly. In her dream, she is going on a trip and excitedly waits for a bus to take her to the cruise ship where friends are gathering. She reaches for her bus ticket, but it's not where she left it in the side pocket of her carry on. She searches her handbag, her pockets, her luggage, but the ticket has vanished. She feels frantic. So much depends on her meeting the ship, meeting her friends, but somehow her ticket has slipped away.

Ellen wakes with a familiar sense of panic and loss. It takes a few seconds for her to realize that what woke her is probably Munroe's truck pulling up in front of his house and not Alistair who may have finally found his way to the cottage. She glances at the clock: four-thirty. She doesn't hear the door of the truck open and close and, just to make sure it's Munroe and not Alistair, she gets up and looks out her window. The light is on in the farmhouse; Ellen can see Lisa moving around the kitchen.

Munroe sits in his truck, the engine off but his hand still resting on the keys in the ignition. He glances at Lisa who looks, just for a second, out the window. He sighs, drops his head back against the headrest thinking that he has two options: he can sleep in his truck or he can go back to Cheri and Mystic Farm. He sees Lisa heading for the door, coming, he thinks, to drag him out of his truck. He turns the key in the ignition, puts the car in reverse and backs onto the paved road just as Lisa appears around the side of the house, hands on hips, watching him drive away.

It's too late for Lisa to go back to bed. Besides, she's already heard one of the twins stirring, probably Grace since Emmy was up not long ago. Lisa casts a glance at Useless Bay, rubs her arms against the frigid morning air, and returns to the house.

Munroe sits at a stop sign, rolls down his window and let's in the damp air coming off of the bay. He turns his truck around. He drives slowly back. He pulls up beside his house, but this time Lisa doesn't look out the window to see him. Grace is up and ready for breakfast. Munroe hesitates, trying to imagine the scene but he is unable to. He turns off the engine, gets out of his truck and goes into the house where he hangs his hat on the hook and leaves his boots by the door. They don't speak. Munroe kisses the top of Grace's head as he passes her on his way to the bedroom. Grace turns in her highchair to watch him go.

It's sad how Lisa and Munroe don't speak when he comes home after being out all night. Lisa is not a fighter. Munroe loves her for that but can't help taking advantage of it. They are incapable of sitting and listening to each other. Surely, Munroe would have told Lisa, or so she thinks, how sorry he was, how much he wanted to be the man she needed, how he had acted out of something…frustration or fear or longing…and that he didn't mean to hurt her but only to preserve himself. Then, Lisa would surely have tried to explain that, no, she didn't really understand what it was like to be a man, to have so much depend on you; she only knows what it's like to be a woman who relies on a man to support his children. Women are afraid, she might say to him, that with small children she could not manage alone and he is her best hope, her only hope, to raise good children who feel loved and secure. She herself wants to feel loved and secure. But they don't talk.

Munroe stirs from the bed around noon. Lisa naps on the couch when she can, Emmy and Grace still demanding her time, infants in their selfish little world, acting without mercy, aware of no situation but their own. She feeds and bathes the girls and they play until Lisa puts them in their cribs for a nap.

As Munroe hesitated in his car the night before, his hand on the ignition key ready to start his engine again, now he rests lazily in bed smoking, knowing that Lisa will not come in, knowing that she will not confront him. Still, he has to get up. There's wood to chop and llamas to feed. He promised his neighbor who'd gone to Tacoma to be with his ailing mother that he'd milk Miss January, his ewe, and deliver the milk to the co-op for the ladies there to make into yogurt. He has a day's work ahead of him and the day is half gone.

Lisa hears Munroe in the bathroom. Emmy wakes up with a diaper that needs changed. Lisa goes into the girl's room and closes the door behind her.

Munroe sees the living room and kitchen deserted and the door to the nursery closed. He thinks about knocking, telling Lisa he's got some work to do but, looking again at the closed door, leaves without saying anything.

Lisa and Munroe had married when Munroe was thirty-four and Lisa was thirty. It was the first marriage for Lisa but the second for Munroe, his first marriage short and childless. He had joined the Navy right after high school, married a woman he'd met in San Diego, and when they split, Munroe came back to Whidbey Island.

When Munroe comes home again, it's already dark. The girls are down for the night. Lisa sits at the kitchen table, coffee gone cold in its cup. She doesn't turn when she hears the door. She simply whispers, "Munroe."

He pulls out the kitchen chair and lets his body fall heavily into it. After a minute, he starts unlacing his work boots.

Lisa thought long and hard all day about what she might say to Munroe but now, looking into his tired face, everything she planned sounds too hostile, too angry. She can hardly keep her hand from touching that tired face and then she does let her hand float up, smiling at the bristles that touch her soft palm, "I love you, you know," she says.

Munroe freezes. Lisa can't fathom what is on her husband's mind. Maybe he's thinking that women think love solves everything. Or maybe he's thinking what a mess he's in. Maybe he thinks that he loves his two baby girls and that they need a mama, but does their mama have to be Lisa? Maybe he thinks about the axe just outside the door. Maybe he thinks of his own mother. Maybe he wonders what he's done. Maybe he feels bad.

"I know you do, Lisa," he says not unkindly, almost regretfully.

Lisa withdraws her hand, drops it in her lap.

They sit there for a minute in stunned silence. Then, Munroe gets up and goes to the bedroom.

Life is hard, Lisa thinks, not just for Munroe who struggles against what is, but for everybody. Life is hard for everybody and once you accept that, a lot more things make sense. Munroe isn't making Lisa's life hard. Life is just hard.

Ellen waits for a second day and a third, meeting every ferry that might carry Alistair. She wishes she had the nerve to call his wife, to ask if anything has happened to him, to ask if she knows where he is, but that's not possible. She keeps her phone on the café table next to the book she's reading. She tells herself that if he doesn't come today, she will go home. Maybe, this time, she can move on.

About the Author

Jo Rousseau graduated from Washington University in St. Louis's Writers Program and Queens University's Book Development Program in Charlotte North Carolina. Her publications includes stories in Stanford University's Literary Imagination, first place in Seattle Magazine's short story competition, first place in Chatter House's essay competition, among others. She currently lives in St. Louis, Missouri where she is working on a novel. This is her second collection of short stories.

Also by ReadLips Press

How to Throw a Psychic a Surprise Party
By Noreen Lace

October Twilight
By Ron Terranova

Swimming Middle River
By Leah Holbrook Sackett

Made in the USA
Monee, IL
23 March 2021